AN UNEQUAL MARRIAGE

Pride and Prejudice Continued

Emma Tennant

sceptre

First published in 1994 by Sceptre Books
An imprint of Hodder and Stoughton
A division of Hodder Headline PLC

10 9 8 7 6 5 4 3 2 1

British Library Cataloguing in Publication Data

Tennant, Emma
Unequal Marriage: Pemberley Continued –
A Sequel to Pride and Prejudice
I. Title
823.914 [F]

ISBN 0 340 61353 X

Typeset by Hewer Text Composition Services, Edinburgh
Printed and bound in Great Britain by Mackays of Chatham plc

Hodder and Stoughton Ltd,
A division of Hodder Headline PLC
338 Euston Road
London NW1 3BH

For Antonia
with love

Part One

One

It is an opinion often expressed, that children come as a blessing to a marriage.

However mixed the blessing may turn out to be, this opinion is so well fixed in people's minds that a deficiency in the offspring of one family or another becomes a matter of disproportionate interest; and never more so than when a man of good fortune and his inheritance are concerned.

So Mrs Bennet, advancing now in years, if not in the dignity and distinction that should accompany old age, was to find on the occasion of the birthday of her grandson Master Edward Darcy.

"My dear Mrs Bennet," said Mrs Long, who had come to Meryton Lodge to visit her friend of many years' standing, "this is not an inconvenient time, I hope! For I recalled even as I set out that today is a holiday indeed, a feast-day, one might say. The fruit of the marriage of your daughter Elizabeth to Mr Darcy must not go ignored, on so propitious a date – even if there has been a slow and uncertain ripening! No differences within the family must impede a young man's expectation of pure pleasure and tokens of affection proffered and gratefully received!"

Mrs Bennet professed to be unaware of Mrs Long's meaning. "It is midsummer, my dear Mrs Long; the heat has been a little much for you, I fear. Meryton Lodge is not a great distance to come on foot – and the trees dear Mr Darcy planted for the comfort and convenience of their shade are of seventeen years' growth. But you have caught the heat a little, I fear, Mrs Long." And Mrs Bennet rang for cool lemonade, which was quickly brought.

Mrs Long, however, continued to protest that she was unaffected by the summer weather, and that she would hope for it to grow even hotter, if it wished.

"My friends and acquaintance", Mrs Long resumed when she had taken a sip of the drink, "have become extremely numerous. True, there are some" – and here she glanced at Mrs Bennet – "who have departed this earth, their life-span achieved . . ."

"You have many years ahead of you, Mrs Long," said Mrs Bennet, who could not imagine where this conversation was leading.

"But for every friend of my youth I must now add two further generations," continued Mrs Long; "and for this reason I keep always by me a book of days. I hope I can recommend you to do the same, Mrs Bennet!"

"I have my own agenda," said Mrs Bennet, "and in it I record my appointments. I would not be surprised to hear you did the same, Mrs Long."

"I have no difficulty in recalling appointments," said Mrs Long; "but I cannot be expected to recall each birthday, each beginning and ending of a school term, and each sacred anniversary of the demise of a dear friend!" At this Mrs Long wiped her eyes, while looking intently at Mrs Bennet as she did so.

A silence now fell in the room, Mrs Bennet's bowed head giving indication of tender thoughts for those once loved and now irremediably lost.

"It is certain that Mr Bennet was interred at Meryton Church eighteen years past. On Michaelmas Day," said Mrs Bennet, as she went into this train of thought with greater interest. "And dear Mary – why, it was six years in April that she died of her consumption and left poor Mr Roper an inconsolable widower."

"Very true, I'm sure," said Mrs Long. "But you dwell on the sad losses you have suffered, Mrs Bennet, and not on the happy celebrations of the present day – this very day, indeed!"

Mrs Bennet went over to the window at this, and remarked

4

she could think of no better way to celebrate a summer's day than to go out and look at the roses, which she proposed to Mrs Long she should do immediately.

"If you had a calendar as well marked as I," said Mrs Long, who could no longer be detained from her purpose, "you would see today as the birthday – the sixteenth birthday, no less! – of your grandson, Mrs Bennet! Your own grandson! I must confess I came here today partly in the hope of finding Master Darcy a guest at Meryton Lodge – with his dear mother Elizabeth and her devoted spouse, Mr Fitzwilliam Darcy! Mr and Mrs Darcy do come down from Derbyshire at this time of year: you have often told me of it, Mrs Bennet – when they travel to their Welsh estates, or to the Continent. You have remarked on frequent occasions that the detour is well worth the making, if the reward is a visit to the grandmother of the heir to Pemberley!"

Mrs Bennet replied that Edward was at school, and in any case her daughter and son-in-law were not accustomed to leave Pemberley until August at the earliest.

"Edward cannot be at school," said Mrs Long triumphantly. "It is the Eton exeat, Mrs Bennet. You would see this yourself if you filled in your calendar as I do."

Mrs Bennet now had nowhere to turn; and Mrs Long, beginning to feel sorry for her, fell back on a subject well worn between them, that of the frequency or infrequency of invitations to Mrs Bennet to visit Pemberley.

"You may say you find the journey fatiguing in the extreme," said Mrs Long, "but Lady Catherine de Bourgh is as advanced in years as you are, my dear Mrs Bennet – and I have heard from Mr Collins that she goes as often as she pleases to Pemberley, to see her nephew Mr Darcy. Surely, Mrs Bennet" – and here Mrs Long became herself agitated and walked about the room, almost colliding with her hostess – "surely, in these difficult times, your daughter needs you: needs the superior wisdom of an older woman, her own mother! I am astonished you are not on your way there now – to be there on the occasion of your grandson's birthday, at least!"

"I shall visit or entertain my relations when I please," cried Mrs Bennet. "Nor does it serve to listen to all Mr Collins has to say, Mrs Long. He exaggerates the number of visits Lady Catherine makes, I have no doubt of it! Mr Collins would do more for her ladyship than for his own daughters, I fear – and poor Charlotte knows it!"

"Poor Charlotte has only daughters," said Mrs Long, who could be put off no longer in her quest for recent information on the character of young Master Darcy. "But *your* daughter is the proud mother of a son!"

"I do think sometimes," said Mrs Bennet, "that there must be a spirit at Longbourn which brings forth only daughters! Mrs Collins will find herself in the identical situation to poor Mrs Bennet: four daughters and Longbourn passing in entail to a stranger nobody knows!"

Mrs Bennet here took a handkerchief from the pocket of her dress and wiped her eyes.

"This has not happened at Pemberley," said Mrs Long. "I only enquire of the progress of young Edward for the sake of the future of that great estate, Mrs Bennet! For – and I recall your telling me this so clearly – when Master Darcy was little more than seven years old and at his first history lessons, he fancied himself fighting the English as a soldier on the side of Napoleon! Do you recall this, Mrs Bennet? It was strange – even as a childish game – for he would have been set against his own father in that case, would he not, in the event of battle?"

Mrs Bennet, after much sighing, said it would have been the case indeed.

Two

Mrs Bennet chose to accompany her friend as far as the gates of Meryton Lodge, before bidding her farewell and making her way to Longbourn. A visit to her old home had been proposed by Charlotte some days ago; the day was mild, with a bright sun making a stroll under trees a pleasant necessity; and, if it had not been for thoughts of Mrs Long and her calendar, the excursion would have been perfect in every way.

It was seven years at least since Edward Darcy had demonstrated the peculiar sympathies so well recalled by Mrs Long this afternoon; and Mrs Bennet could be forgiven for feeling it was seven times as long again that she had repented her foolish confidence to her friend. A Christmas visit to Pemberley had provided Mrs Bennet with her first glimpse of the oddness of the child. She had tried, as she was wont to remind herself frequently, to voice her concerns to her daughter and son-in-law, but these concerns were met with coldness and what appeared to be indifference; and on one occasion, as Mrs Bennet was never to forget, she had been forcibly escorted from the long gallery, in the presence of Lady Catherine de Bourgh, by Mr Darcy himself.

It was true that an eight-year-old boy might entertain fantasies of fighting on the side of Bonaparte in the Peninsular Wars simply to be unlike his schoolfellows; but, as Mrs Bennet had informed Mrs Long on her return to Meryton, Edward had no schoolfellows for the very simple reason that Mr Darcy, as befitted a man of his rank and fortune, had not sent him away to school. A tutor was at Pemberley; he had instructed Edward in logic, moral and metaphysics; and had prepared

7

him for Eton, where he had by now been a pupil for the past four years. There had been no reports of any trouble since; but the fact that the lad had on arrival apparently attempted to assume a name other than Darcy was known to Mrs Bennet after eavesdropping a conversation between her daughters at Pemberley on the occasion of another visit planned to coincide with the festive season. Even though she had not passed on this disturbing information to Mrs Long, Mrs Bennet had for some time strongly felt the need for a confidante on the subject of her grandson. Certainly, in the years that had gone by since Edward had been admitted to Eton College, she had heard no rumour of any ill-doings on the part of the lad; that it was two years since she had been invited as a guest to Pemberley remained unconnected for her with the occasion of making a comment, not kindly received, on the subject of her grandson. Mrs Long's calendar doubtless recorded the length of the lapse. But, as Mrs Bennet could and did reiterate, she was accustomed to receive letters of great substance from her daughter; and "when I want to see the Darcys I go to the delightful house in Holland Park that Mr Darcy built for me so that I might bring out dear Kitty into society".

Mrs Bennet had of course done no such thing, for she knew Elizabeth and her son-in-law were too well content and occupied at Pemberley to visit London; but Kitty was married, and living in Sussex with her husband, a Major Courtauld; and Mrs Bennet liked to regale Mrs Long as well as her daughter Elizabeth's friend Mrs Collins with tales of the splendid season which had resulted in a match equally satisfactory. That all was entirely harmonious with the Darcys was a creed with Mrs Bennet, and she wondered again at her ancient indiscretion to Mrs Long, as she reached the palings of her old home. To confide in dear Charlotte was out of the question, of course; but the uncanny span of Mrs Long's memory awakened fresh anxiety, as well as indignation at the suggestion made by her own grandson that his grandmother was French. He would have grown out of the conceit by now, surely – yet Mrs Bennet felt as never before the need to be reassured on the subject of the future master of Pemberley.

Mr Collins, having greeted Mrs Bennet as she stepped up to the door, soon bustled to show off the latest improvements at Longbourn, and thoughts of Mrs Long and her calendar were soon replaced by further irritations. "You will observe, dear Mrs Bennet, that I have opened up the west wall of the library so that one may walk out into a conservatory. At night, book in hand, it is possible to gaze at the galaxy and to reflect on the brevity of life, the vanity of possessions and the meaning of the universe. Charlotte would place palm trees and go in for gilding and plastering; but we are not at Brighton here, as I tell her, we are in the house of a man of the cloth. All this is mine; but it will not be so for ever, for I will be called to the mansion of the Lord."

Charlotte came in and attended to Mrs Bennet with sweetness, asking her for news of Elizabeth; and of the Bingleys also, and their numerous progeny.

Mrs Bennet replied that they were all in excellent health.

"I hear that dear Elizabeth sets up her own dairy herd at Pemberley," said Charlotte, when she had shown Mrs Bennet to a chair in the conservatory; "and that she has the best cream and butter in the country! She is an excellent manager; I always knew she would be; I am so happy for her, Mrs Bennet!"

Mrs Bennet, although disconcerted by the large expanse of glass which surrounded her in this new room that was the ruin of Mr Bennet's excellent library, was pleased to hear this and paused gravely while attempting to return such sentiments in kind. "And how are your daughters, my dear Charlotte?" was all she could manage in the end. "You must look forward to the day when they each meet an eligible husband, I dare say!"

"They are young for that yet," said Charlotte, laughing. "We are all as happy as can be, Mrs Bennet." And she proceeded to enumerate the qualities and accomplishments of all four of her daughters, while Mr Collins, affecting modesty and reticence, walked from the conservatory into the garden to examine his new saplings.

"I feel sorry for you, poor Charlotte," said Mrs Bennet, despite this litany of delight, "for you are in an identical situation to mine. Longbourn will pass to a cousin – you will have nothing to leave your daughters. Of course, I had five and you have four. But I now have only four, since the loss of my poor Mary."

"Her death was tragic indeed," said Charlotte in a low voice.

"Her relict, Mr Thomas Roper, is inconsolable. There is no other woman so scholarly as Mary; there can be no successor, for him."

Charlotte showed surprise at the suggestion that Mrs Bennet was closely attuned to the feelings and prospects in marriage of Mr Thomas Roper.

"He has written to me. He has shown great fortitude, in accepting he cannot be heir to Pemberley. I believe there are *some* male cousins, when a house and estate are in entail" – and here Mrs Bennet lowered her voice, at the imminent re-entry of Mr Collins into the conservatory – "as is the case, as you well know, with both Pemberley and Longbourn – who become embittered in the extreme, when an heir is born and supplants them."

"Indeed," said Charlotte. Her thoughts could be observed to move in the direction Mrs Bennet had secretly intended, and she now asked in the kindest manner of the progress of young Edward.

"He must take every care," said Mr Collins, who was now within earshot and advancing on Charlotte and Mrs Bennet. "I have heard there is a coterie at Eton which can only be described as evil. Young Edward must be most vigilant, to escape their clutches."

"Evil?" asked Mrs Bennet. "Surely that cannot be possible, at so eminent a place of learning?"

"There are negligent parents in every walk of life," said Mr Collins, who now darted a keen glance at Mrs Bennet, refreshing an anxious thought of some years' duration, namely that Mrs Long had confided in Charlotte and Mr Collins the nature of young Edward's wayward loyalties.

"The most powerful and wealthy in the land may be less able to rear a child in the knowledge of right and wrong than a humble labourer!"

Mrs Bennet was silenced by this, and the climate of conversation was altered only by the arrival of Amy, Charlotte's second daughter, who was indeed as pretty, modest and intelligent as a young girl of fourteen brought up quietly in the country could be expected to be. Mrs Bennet was soon prattling of the pleasures which lay ahead for Amy, as a result of the grand connections now held by the widow of Mr Bennet.

"You shall meet my grandson Edward Darcy, my dear child. I have a house in London, at Holland Park, I would have you know, and next year will be the occasion for a ball for my granddaughter Miranda, who is Edward's senior by a year. You will be too young to come – unless your dear Mama is very lenient with you – but you shall have a ball of your own when the time comes. What would you say to that, dear Amy?"

"Both Amy and her elder sister will be entertained by Lady Catherine de Bourgh at Rosings, when they are of an age to enter society," said Mr Collins before his daughter could make any reply to Mrs Bennet's offer. "Lady Catherine will ensure they are introduced to everyone of consequence. I dare say there will be dancing."

"Mr Collins, this is the first I have heard of it!" cried Charlotte. "But we must not talk of *our* children. I so much hoped, when Mrs Bennet was kind enough to agree to pay us a visit at Longbourn, that we would hear more of dear Elizabeth's family! How Edward shapes – how he does at school – where Miranda's talents and accomplishments will lead her –"

"They can lead her somewhere better, I trust, than the post of governess to someone else's children," said Amy, with a suddenness which took the company by surprise.

"Amy, you will leave the conservatory," said Mr Collins, "and look to your lessons. You will be fortunate indeed, to find any decent family offering you the post of governess, if you keep such a sharp tongue in your head."

"She is young," said Charlotte, who was unable to resist a smile. "You know, Mrs Bennet, she often brings dear Lizzy to mind, when *she* was a girl. How I do miss her – she is far too far away from Hertfordshire."

"She may be in need of your counsel and support, Charlotte," said Mr Collins in a very solemn tone. "I give full permission for you to visit Pemberley, and would have granted it some years ago when first I heard the rumours – not that I hearken to such things as rumours, naturally –"

"What rumours were these?" cried Mrs Bennet, despite herself eager to glean the full extent of Mr Collins's knowledge.

"– And it must also be noted that Mrs Collins and I have left Longbourn solely to pay the attentions to Lady Catherine which her advancing years demand. Charlotte is a dutiful mother; her daughters are young still, but could sustain her absence by now. Charlotte, I accept that you should visit your old friend Mrs Darcy at Pemberley. I may join you later."

Mrs Bennet could receive no further information on the subject of the rumours, try as she might; and after a short while she accepted the offer of Mr Collins's pony and trap to carry her back to Meryton Lodge, for it was generally agreed that the day had become considerably warmer since the time of her arrival at Longbourn.

Three

Elizabeth and Darcy, after nineteen years of marriage, still were considered the most fortunate couple in Derbyshire – and beyond; for tales of the beauty and intelligence of Mrs Darcy, the joys of Pemberley and the agreeable character of the owner of this great house and estate travelled with every guest who took their leave well satisfied with their sojourn there.

Mrs Darcy, it was generally accorded, had every blessing a provident deity could bestow: a daughter, who took after her mother, with her fine eyes and her open disposition; a son who was said by some to be the image of Lady Anne, Mr Darcy's mother – though others found this observation ill mannered, as it only served to draw attention to his stature, which was certainly limited; and friends and admiring acquaintances without number. Jane Bingley, despite all the new faces in the county who might have superseded her in Elizabeth's affections, remained closer than any other person – save her husband – to her sister, and when confidences were exchanged between the two women, still youthful and in the full bloom of contentment and motherhood, it was easy to recall Miss Bennet and Elizabeth Bennet as girls, understanding and caring for the other under Mrs Bennet's impractical eye, at Longbourn. Jane had now five children – and was not "worn out at thirty" as had been foreseen by Darcy's aunt, Lady Catherine de Bourgh, on the occasion of her first visit to Pemberley since the marriage of which she so disapproved. On the contrary, Jane, for all her busy life with her children, had become an excellent weaver of tapestries – some of which were on show at Pemberley, to the delight of guests – whereas Lady Catherine's own daughter Miss de Bourgh, who had refused many offers to enter the matrimonial state, had few pastimes but her music, and a countenance more weathered by the passing of the years than Mrs Bingley. Elizabeth – and here it was agreed that it seemed as if a magical charm had been placed upon her at birth – was noted to be younger and lovelier with each year that passed.

Mr Darcy showed his appreciation of this by growing, in turn, more amenable each year to his wife's wishes and suggestions; and he had come to learn that what might pass for a whim, to be granted on grounds of the irresistible character of his wife, was always in fact a shrewd investment as well as a thing of beauty. Elizabeth had filled the drawing-rooms and galleries of Pemberley with paintings by Bonington and Constable, and the watery light of Turner shone in contrast to the old portraits on the walls by Van Dyck and Titian. A sense of a new age, inspired by sparkling gaiety and by the genius of Elizabeth Darcy herself, imbued the house and garden and parkland of Pemberley, so that no visitor could fail to observe the felicity of the new installations and their relationship with Nature. The ornamental lake, which Darcy had at first opposed, was now his favourite spot of a summer evening; and here, despite the midges, he sat night after night with his Lizzy's uncle Gardiner, when that venerable old man came to fish. The herd of Jersey cows, with their bright brown flanks, he now saw as a complement to Pemberley; and the little milking-parlour, where the village children could sit among picturesque ruins and enjoy picnics with the mistress of the house and her daughter Miranda, brought residents and working people of Pemberley together in the summer months. All in all, the place provided an idyll for those who came there; and the consensus of opinion was that Mrs Darcy must take responsibility for the harmony and success of the enterprise that was Pemberley. It was whispered that even Lady Catherine had expressed her approval – but only to her nephew, naturally, and in the strictest confidence.

This summer was to see the marriage of one of the Darcys'

oldest friends, a cousin of Mr Darcy, Colonel Fitzwilliam. That he had once been on the brink of proposing marriage to Elizabeth – when Mr Darcy had seemed an odious person to her, though it was hard for her to recall this now – served to strengthen the tie between all three. It was said that Colonel Fitzwilliam had long nursed a broken heart, since Miss Elizabeth Bennet's discovery that Mr Darcy was not quite the villain he had been made out to be. That she had fallen into the arms of a man so much the superior of the kindly colonel could not surprise; but it was said, also, that it was for this reason that he had come to live a few miles from Pemberley, on the edge of moorland, where he set himself up as a hill farmer, though clearly very much a gentleman farmer of a better kind than the name would normally suggest. He was not rich; but he counted as his fortune the catching of a glimpse of Mrs Darcy as she went about her business in her milking-parlour, or in her wild garden, where water was trained to fall through mossy glades, bordered by primulas and shrubs of exquisite variety. For all that he was a nurseryman, a gardener of skill and a countryman with an infinite degree of patience – which certainly Mr Darcy had not – Colonel Fitzwilliam did not have it in him to correct his cousin, when he was proud, or to show his lifelong loyalty to his cousin's wife. Only his eyes and blushes gave him away – when Mrs Darcy came out of the wood suddenly and discovered him standing there, gazing at her; or when she and Darcy, so seldom left alone in all the bustle and administration of a great place such as Pemberley, stopped in a glade and, thinking themselves quite alone, allowed themselves to speak fond words in a manner not possible when under the scrutiny of servants, children and guests. That Colonel Fitzwilliam was perfectly well tolerated, if he did happen to be in the way of a couple so passionately in love after all these years, served to demonstrate that he was none of the former: he was friend, defender and permanent courtier – and both Darcys liked him all the more for it.

Colonel Fitzwilliam's marriage, therefore, coming as it did out of the blue, caused some amazement at Pemberley.

Elizabeth and Jane talked of it, in Elizabeth's boudoir, a room with a little fireplace set with Delft tiles of bright white and blue – a room so altogether like her sister in its brilliance, softness and clarity of look, that Jane would say often how much she preferred to sit there, to passing time in the grander salons and state rooms downstairs.

The wedding was due to take place within the week. The chapel on the estate had been bedecked by Elizabeth with greenery; and this would be supplemented by the flowers of the garden, in abundant generosity. Elizabeth had a design of old roses, and delphiniums, and sweet-williams by the score, to bring on the colonel's blushes. She had decided on giving a fine wedding to her old friend. There would be a ball, and dancing, and some of Mr Darcy's best wines, brought up out of the cellar in preparation. The Ming vases would adorn the altar, and would be filled with bouquets of white rosebuds. All this, as Jane remarked in Elizabeth's boudoir, for a man at least the age of Mr Darcy, and a confirmed bachelor all his life! Was it not strange, that he should fall so precipitately in love, and with someone so many years his junior?

"We have not met his bride," said Elizabeth, "but you will not be astonished to hear, my sweet Jane, that Lady Catherine, as aunt to Colonel Fitzwilliam as well as to Darcy, has studied the genealogy of the future spouse of Colonel Fitzwilliam most earnestly. Lady Sophia Farquhar is, as we are all made aware on every possible occasion, the daughter of a Scottish earl – and, according to Lady Catherine, both he and Lady Sophia's mother, the late countess, would have wished for nothing better than the nuptials of their daughter and Colonel Fitzwilliam."

"But why does not the earl give away his daughter?" asked Jane.

"Did you not hear Lady Catherine in the long gallery yesterday evening?" said Elizabeth, laughing. "The earl also is deceased. His estates have passed to a nephew, who has returned from the colonies to find himself in this enviable position; and Lady Sophia, being a complete stranger to her kinsman, prefers to marry in the simplicity of the chapel at Pemberley."

"Simplicity?" said Jane, wondering. "Surely, she cannot have come here, Lizzy?"

"I heard she did," said Elizabeth, "when Darcy and I were in Wales, some months ago. Colonel Fitzwilliam reported that Lady Sophia liked the charm of Pemberley, and the economy of line as well as dimension."

"Heavens!" cried Jane, who was now more amazed than she had been at the start of the conversation by Colonel Fitzwilliam's choice of wife. "Where can she have spent her youth, if she finds Pemberley small? How can Colonel Fitzwilliam provide for her, in his humble farmhouse?"

At this, both sisters burst out laughing again; and only the approaching footsteps of Mr Darcy caused them to assume grave expressions.

"We must pray that Lady Catherine does not hear of her new kinswoman's idea of scale," whispered Jane, despite Mr Darcy's putting his head round the door and smiling very genially as he did so. "And I'm sure I do hope he will be as much with you here, dear Lizzy, after his marriage, as he was before. Without him, a harder time would have been had with Edward, so I have often thought . . ."

Here Jane broke off, and started to colour, for she was seldom without tact and, with her acutely sensitive nature, could see that Elizabeth and Darcy both looked away and were at pains to set off on another subject.

"It seems we will have a fine day for the wedding," said Mr Darcy.

"I have spoken to McGregor about the greenhouses," said Elizabeth, "and he cannot promise peaches before we go south – though he could promise strawberries for the wedding supper."

Jane rose, and was about to leave the room when Elizabeth begged her to stay a moment longer with them. "For I am so happy, dear Jane, and I wish you to share in my happiness!" Here Elizabeth glanced at Darcy, as if to ask his permission, and to grant him hers, simultaneously. "We have heard, quite simply, that there is good news from Eton. Edward has performed well. He has gained distinction as a scholar. We received a letter from him to that effect – and, to reward him, Darcy permits that he comes to Pemberley for the wedding!"

"It is the exeat this week," said Darcy, smiling at his wife's evident joy and barely able to conceal his own. "We expect him any moment. He will be with us for dinner if he does not idle over a choice of cravats before he departs!"

"I am sure he will come directly," said Elizabeth, with a note of anxiety that was only too detectable to Jane.

"And dear Mr Falk – he must be overjoyed!" cried Jane, to cover the brief silence that had now fallen between Edward's mother and father. "How proud he must be, of all the effort he put towards dear Edward's education."

"He was at first unable to believe the news," said Elizabeth.

"Mr Falk has been invaluable as tutor to all our children," said Jane, for she felt still a constraint between her sister and Mr Darcy. "It is due to your kindness, Lizzy – and your generosity, Darcy – that he stays on at Pemberley and must never feel the pinch of poverty or the loneliness of old age!"

"There is room enough at Pemberley for Mr Falk," said Darcy, whose good humour had returned in full. "Though he has become over-fond of airing his views, I fear."

Jane and Elizabeth exchanged glances at this, and concealed as well they could their own smiles of satisfaction and contentment. For the early years of Elizabeth and Darcy's marriage would not have known such ease of manner on the part of the proud master of Pemberley: he would have shown a politeness bordering on the icy when it came to tolerating the company of his son's tutor – and would have shown him the door once the studies undertaken had been completed. That he had not, Jane knew, was a result of the benign influence of her sister – Lizzy had softened Mr Darcy, and enabled him to show benevolence, when his nature had since he was a child been blighted by a coldness imbued by his aunt Lady Catherine and others of the grand family to which his mother had belonged. Elizabeth was so lacking in pretension and guile that she refused obeisances from the workers on the estate – and insisted their children should play with hers in the long galleries and passages of Pemberley, despite the invaluable pictures and porcelain assembled there. She it was who could claim responsibility for the rapidity with which Darcy could change mood, laugh and smile again, as he would never have been capable at the outset of their marriage.

There had been a time when this was not the case. Edward's early years had been difficult indeed – he had been a strange little child, as even Mrs Reynolds, the loyal housekeeper, had admitted to a few chosen friends in the servants' hall at Pemberley. It seemed impossible that he would one day inherit. And he had given vent to outbursts of temper so violent and uncontrollable that a nurse and two nursemaids had been unable to restrain him. In Jane's secret opinion, it was Mr Darcy's treatment of his son on these occasions which had led to his succeeding crimes – those of deviousness and deceit – for Mr Darcy had punished the lad severely and confined him to his room on a diet of bread and water. Elizabeth had begged her husband to show leniency; but Mr Darcy could not and would not; and, by the time Edward reached the age of seven, his illiteracy and ungovernable nature had rendered the engaging of an instructor and monitor inevitable, for the young heir to all Mr Darcy held and owned. Edward must have a tutor – and Jane had seen Elizabeth's vast relief at her dawning apprehension of the nature of Mr Falk – who could show strictness when his employer was in the vicinity, but who was otherwise a model of kindness and understanding towards the child. By then, however, a very large measure of these qualities was urgently required.

Edward shocked a Christmas gathering at Pemberley, in his eighth year, by pulling out a box of soldiers and announcing he was on the side of the army of Napoleon and would beat any of his young cousins at war. He went on, later in the visit of his grandmother Mrs Bennet and his great-aunt Lady Catherine, to be discovered to have informed Mr Falk that his grandmother's antecedents were French – and poor Mr Falk it was who had to suffer the ridicule of the company when he courteously enquired of Mrs Bennet if her name was to be sounded with a hard or soft "t" at the end of it.

Jane's cheeks burned, when she recalled these things, both for Elizabeth and for herself. There *had* been a Frenchwoman, all those years ago – she had been the mistress of her own dear husband Charles, but long before Mr Bingley had rented Netherfield, near Longbourn, and had fallen sincerely in love with Jane. The child of Mr Bingley, once owned and accepted by Jane in the kindness of her heart, had gone on well, and had entered the militia of a neighbouring county. And this in itself, as Jane was so keenly aware, made Edward's unfortunate character all the harder for Elizabeth to bear.

Now, after Mr Falk's period of tuition and guidance, all had been well for many years. True, in the holidays at Mr Darcy's Yorkshire estate just a few summers ago, the lad had gone off with the beaters rather than stay with the gentry, at the grouse shoot – and had been found late at night asleep in a barn and distinctly the worse for drink. But he had been thirteen years old; and Elizabeth had persuaded her husband to give his son a good lecture, rather than punishment that involved a more public humiliation.

Since then, the boy had given no offence at Eton; and reports of his scholastic progress, though inclined to be monotonous, were fairly good. Elizabeth and Darcy relaxed their guard; for keeping their anxieties to themselves, with all the attendant strain and pretence, had many times endangered their marriage. Now they were delighted at Jane's approval of their encouragement to their son, that as a reward for his efforts Edward was to be allowed to come to Derbyshire for the marriage of Colonel Fitzwilliam.

Edward Darcy had been taught all he knew of sport by his kindly cousin, and was by now an excellent shot and a fine fisherman. Colonel Fitzwilliam's strength and patience, both Jane and Elizabeth knew, had contributed greatly to the improvement of the character of the young heir; and that Darcy was also prepared to concede the importance of his friend in the rearing of the lad was evident from his determination that Edward should come north for the event.

Elizabeth and Darcy went off smiling, in different directions, to find the gardener and complete arrangements for the nuptial day, and Jane made her way also to find her husband as he walked about the park at Pemberley with their youngest daughter. She reflected as she went that she was not worldly – she would say, with Elizabeth, that she cared not at all for the opinion of those, like Lady Catherine de Bourgh and Miss Caroline Bingley, who lived to see the faults in others and speak spitefully of them. But she was happy that Mr Darcy's aunt and Charles's sister would be of the party for the marriage of Colonel Fitzwilliam. They would see for themselves how Master Darcy had prospered, when they had expressed grave doubts as to the boy's suitability as heir to Pemberley.

Four

There was much to be done before the celebration of the marriage of Colonel Fitzwilliam and Lady Sophia – and among the most pressing concerns was the comfort of the bride, who came later in the day with Lady Catherine de Bourgh, to spend the brief period leading up to the consecration of holy vows as the guest of Mr and Mrs Fitzwilliam Darcy at Pemberley.

The groom would attend an evening party in celebration of the forthcoming union, before the great day itself; and flowers, champagne and a fine dinner were still in the process of arrangement; there was the matter of Lady Sophia's bedchamber, which Elizabeth intended to bedeck with the sweetest flowers from the garden, choosing only yellow and white as the bridal theme; and there were, besides, manifold little tasks which needed attention, for there was to be quite a throng at Pemberley, comprising both the guests in the house and those who came from afar to toast the couple after the joining together in matrimony of Darcy's loyal cousin and his betrothed.

Elizabeth hurried away from her boudoir, therefore, with a host of details coming in at her from every quarter. Her first assistant in all these matters would be Miranda – and Elizabeth knew where she would find her, for the girl was seldom inclined to stay indoors. Miranda loved the open air, and the development of the projects she and her mother had put in train together, more than domesticity or the perfecting of the usual accomplishments expected of a young lady. The model dairy, on the outskirts of the park by the side of the Pemberley estate nearest to the village, was the site of a prospering experiment with a herd of Jersey cows; and it was here that Miranda, who was strong and tall for her seventeen years, liked to spend the majority of her time. That she would happily assist her mother in chores connected with the minutiae of running a household such as Pemberley was, however, without doubt. Miranda was known by all to be lacking entirely in egotism and vanity. She would generously give to Elizabeth all the assistance and encouragement required for the welcoming to Pemberley of Colonel Fitzwilliam's bride – and, if she sensed sometimes that these entertainments were a trial to her mother, she was not slow to demonstrate her sympathy and understanding, even if, by reason of her youth, she could never know the shyness her mother had suffered, when first finding herself chatelaine of Pemberley and hostess to the likes of Lady Catherine de Bourgh.

Elizabeth was surprised, as she made her way across the park, to find footsteps hurrying after her; and finally a firm arm taking hers. She slowed her pace, and smiled. Even after all these years it was a pleasure to hear Darcy come quickly after her; and she could surmise, by his own smiling expression, that he brought nothing alarming in the way of news.

"Loveliest Elizabeth," said Darcy, as they strolled at a more sedate pace through air scented with all the fragrances a good gardener and an expansive parkland and flower garden could provide, "you work hard for the happiness of our cousin Fitzwilliam. I am happy and proud – for he is a man who would do harm to no one, and who has brought us as much joy and contentment as could be wished from a friend – even if, as I must own, he is a perfect idiot at backgammon, and allows himself to be beaten even by Charles Bingley!"

Elizabeth, laughing, said she would do all she could for a friend who had been retainer, protector and ally, in all the years they had spent together at Pemberley.

"You have shown recognition of my long friendship with Charles Bingley also," said Darcy, "for it is not to your liking to entertain Miss Caroline Bingley, who comes to Pemberley for the wedding; and I did give you my word, sweet Eliza, when we were a short time married, that you would not be imposed upon to act as hostess to Miss Bingley ever again!".

"I am sorry for her," said Elizabeth, in the frank tone her husband had come to love and trust, preferring the company and unceasing honesty of Elizabeth to any flatterer – of which, as the master of Pemberley, he had no lack. "Miss Bingley sees all her acquaintance married, and with children. She is denied every happiness. Fortunate indeed that Charles grants her the dower house at Barlow. But if you must look for charity and compassion, look to my sister Jane!"

The mention of children brought about a silence between Darcy and Elizabeth, and they walked on, in the direction of the model dairy. The outskirts of the village began to be visible, through the trees; and an ancient cottage, with thatch and a cover of bright red roses, made their first stopping point before going another few hundred yards to the farm.

"The house will be re-roofed by harvest-time," said Darcy, who could sense his wife's thoughts by now, before she could voice them. "Have no fear, Elizabeth – I would not risk incurring your displeasure, in the event of your finding old Martin and his wife with the rains coming in on them!"

Elizabeth, looking around and seeing they were enclosed in a glade of elms and thus invisible to the rest of the world, here reached up and thanked her husband with feeling. She knew his good nature could at times be overlaid by severity – or by negligence, even, for he had so much to see to, on the estate, that a tumbledown cottage might escape his attentions for longer than was warranted. She dared to hope that her care, and Darcy's actions, made for good management at Pemberley; and was modestly delighted when this was suggested, in the county.

Miranda, who now had seen her parents and ran towards them from the new wooden building that housed the dairy, had skills that were fast becoming a vital component in the successful handling of the place. The development of new methods of farming, and of modern machinery, was more easily grasped by the girl than by her parents; and, unnoticeably at first, Darcy had come to depend on his daughter for advice and assistance on matters concerning the estate.

"Darcy," said Elizabeth in a quiet voice as Miranda approached, "I am so happy that Edward joins us for the wedding! And I still cannot recover from the news that he has gained distinction as a scholar! We should reward him, further, my love – should we not take him abroad with us? If we do go abroad, for there is the Yorkshire shoot, I know, and then the visit to Brecon, for there is much to oversee in Wales . . ."

"I have granted that Edward takes his exeat with us here, and that is enough for the present," said Darcy, who frowned as always at the excessive indulgence – in his eyes at least – of the mother to her son. "We have seen the results of spoiling him, surely, in the past."

Elizabeth bit her lip at this, and pulled away from him, so that Miranda came on her parents somewhat estranged from each other, and looked enquiringly up at them. That she also sensed the probable reason for the sudden unhappiness of Elizabeth was made manifest in the glance of sympathy she directed at her.

"I was about to inform your mother that I take her to Italy after the marriage festivities of cousin Fitzwilliam are done," said Darcy, who smiled again now, and very gaily. "We shall go to Venice, and pay a visit to our friends at the Palazzo Albrizzi." So saying, and without glancing at his wife, Mr Darcy, still smiling broadly, turned on his heel and made his way back to the house through the park, leaving both wife and daughter staring after him. That Darcy, as Elizabeth confided with a sigh, was happy to reward her for her labours in the cause of Colonel Fitzwilliam's happiness was evident; that Edward would receive recompense for *his*, in the cause of scholarship, was already denied. But as Elizabeth had now to concur, at Miranda's insistence, she had never been to Venice, and knew only that a city built on water must be a wonderful thing.

Five

Elizabeth and Miranda now occupied themselves in the gathering of flowers for the galleries and grand rooms of Pemberley. Elizabeth's simple and informal arrangements were admired by all but Lady Catherine, who deplored the picturesque and remained firmly in the traditions of the past. Elizabeth found yellow, her favourite colour, in the tiger lilies, and white in the lilac she placed together for Lady Sophia's bedchamber, while Miranda provided a centrepiece for the dining table of the marriage feast. The slow selecting of the blooms, on a day when the humming of bees was the only sound in the walled flower garden, brought calm and a desire to talk, if only in a desultory manner; and Elizabeth, despite herself, expressed once more her sorrow that Mr Darcy did not exhibit more pride in his son's recent achievements.

"Papa is careful, while you are too quick, Mama!" said Miranda, laughing. "He is overcome, I have no doubt, by the great improvement in Edward – but he does not like to express his feelings too soon. He wishes to mark this happy time, instead, by taking you to Italy – and you know how you have wished to go there for so many years. Now you *will* go – just think, Mama! And take your sketching-book, if you please, for you sadly neglect your talent."

Elizabeth laughed; but said in a quiet voice that she still felt the lack of reward for Edward: that she would have liked to take him to Italy or France – with Miranda, naturally.

"Mama, you ask for too much!" cried Miranda. "You appear to desire nothing, and yet you want very often the impossible! Papa is not ready yet to make a tour

29

with Edward. The past has been grim, for father and son alike."

"You are wise, Miranda," said Elizabeth sighing; and as she did so she reflected, not for the first time, that they were more like sisters than mother and daughter; while, at times, she had to confess she felt herself Miranda's daughter and their roles entirely the other way about.

"Why do not you take Edward to Wales, when you go, later in the year?" continued Miranda, and then waved her hand in a languid movement to the garden gate – for Mr Gresham, the architect and the son of the bailiff at Pemberley, had just arrived there and stood smiling in at Mrs Darcy and her daughter as they stooped over a bed of blue and yellow violas.

"I could not do that," said Elizabeth, without thinking what she said – then stopped, and coloured, standing and straightening up as Mr Gresham approached, just in time to catch her blushes.

"I cannot for the life of me see why not," said Miranda, who knelt even deeper into a bush of roses let go wild at the express command of Elizabeth and despite the disapproval of McGregor, the head gardener.

Elizabeth was confused, and in this state was particularly youthful and beautiful – in the eyes, certainly, of Mr Gresham, who had come north to Derbyshire for the marriage of his old friend Colonel Fitzwilliam; but also, though he would declare it to no one, to refresh his perennial need to see Mrs Darcy, and spend time in her company. For, if Colonel Fitzwilliam was devoted to Elizabeth – and mindful, ever, of the marriage vows between Darcy and Elizabeth Bennet – Mr Gresham had feelings of a decidedly more uncertain nature on the subject. Mr Gresham had been a young man at the time of the marriage of Elizabeth and Darcy. He had seen the cavalier manner in which Darcy had treated his young bride when she had been tormented by his friends and relations on the occasion of her first Christmas party at Pemberley.

He had witnessed Darcy's pompous and unexplained

departure for London, when Lady Catherine's demand to sit in a room apart from Elizabeth's mother, Mrs Bennet, had driven Elizabeth to extremes of mortification and shame; and he had proposed to Elizabeth that he escort her in her own flight south – though she had gone, in the end, not to London but into the arms of her old friend Charlotte Lucas, married to Mr Collins at Longbourn. Gresham had understood that Elizabeth's discovery that she was with child soon after this had overjoyed her and reconciled her to her husband; but he was unable to see, probably for the very good reason that he did not wish to, that Darcy was as violently in love with his wife as ever; and that Elizabeth was as much in love with her husband, in turn. Had he grasped this, he would have guessed the reason for Elizabeth's blushes more easily – for Elizabeth's sudden knowledge that, despite her suggesting it, she did not really wish to take her son with her to Wales was yet another expression of her preference for time alone with Darcy – when so much of their love had been set necessarily aside in the past by the child. But the architect noted only a look in the eyes of Mrs Darcy which recalled to him those early days at Pemberley when she had needed him for reassurance and companionship.

It was not easy for Mr Gresham to resist the impulse to lean over the box hedge to the path where Elizabeth stood, still bewildered by the sudden intelligence of her greater love for her husband than her son, and take her in his arms. But resist it he did, and distracted himself by pulling out a rose striped in red and white, propagated in the age of Henry VIII, and growing in the walled flower garden at Pemberley ever since. This he handed, with a courtly air, to Miranda – though it seemed improbable that Elizabeth, who had now taken stock of the consistency of his feelings towards her, was deceived by the gesture.

"I come to seek you out, Mrs Darcy," said Mr Gresham, with all the note of restraint proper to the son of the bailiff, and himself past librarian at Pemberley, "to say that some of your guests are arrived – and Mr Darcy is nowhere to be found, either in the house or in the grounds!"

"So soon!" cried Elizabeth and Miranda in unison; and ran to the gate, baskets of flowers in their hands, leaving Mr Gresham bending down in the brick path after them, to pick the blooms that tumbled out in their haste.

Six

Charlotte Collins and Lady Lucas, on determining to postpone no longer calling on Mrs Bennet at Meryton Lodge, and on finding it a very fine day, walked by the side of the town and turned into the back drive in time to see a splendid carriage, with a coat of arms on the side not discernible at this distance from the two ladies, leave the house and go out by the front gates.

"Whoever can that be?" Lady Lucas enquired of her daughter. "That is not Mr Darcy and Elizabeth, surely, visiting Mrs Bennet at this season in the year?"

"I think not," said Charlotte smiling, "for Lizzy would have called on us first at Longbourn, Mama. Some new acquaintance of Mrs Bennet, and we shall shortly discover who it is, I have no doubt."

"If your father were here, he would certainly identify the insignia," declared Lady Lucas. "But he spends so long in London there is little chance he will come down today and recognise them."

Charlotte was about to exclaim that Mrs Bennet would lose no time in delineating the crest of her new visitor, when the lady in question waved from the window and came out on the step without delay.

"I wonder the coach had room enough to come in," said Mrs Bennet, who had little time for greetings from Lady Lucas and her daughter; "the drive here is narrow enough – I beg Mr Darcy to widen it, but this never comes about! I can only hope that no damage befell the passenger when she was thrown from side to side on the loose stones – no one ever comes to mend the road, however much I ask it!"

"I should hope that a passenger of such consequence would escape harm," agreed Lady Lucas, who was astonished at Mrs Bennet's evident preference for carriages over pedestrians. "Perhaps we have called at an inconvenient time, my dear Mrs Bennet, and should try our good fortune at a more expedient moment."

Mrs Bennet continued to stare down the drive as her friend spoke, as if the carriage could be summoned back and disgorge its passenger once more. Charlotte, seeing the call was inopportune indeed, touched her mother's sleeve. "You know the midday sun does not suit you, Mama – and, besides, Mr Collins needs me in the *potager* – he has threatened to dig up the beans today and replace them with peas, if I am not there to assist him!"

None of this was heard by Lady Lucas, who was now set on the satisfaction of her curiosity. Her entry into the house was followed, if reluctantly, by her daughter and Mrs Bennet.

"I thought to bring you news of the court of St James," said Lady Lucas without preamble, on reaching the parlour and seating herself in a chair. "Sir William writes that the Queen is pleasant, but exceedingly dull. I have heard there are young women who have been through six or seven seasons without finding a husband, Mrs Bennet! The court offers nothing to the young – there is so little to amuse – and there is a great dearth of partners!"

Mrs Bennet remarked that she had no anxieties on that score. "Miranda is as beautiful as my Lizzy, Lady Lucas. And naturally her position as the daughter of Mr Darcy of Pemberley will make her a great catch! It will be more a question, my dear Lady Lucas, of beating away the admirers from her door!"

"She cannot be expected to bring any great dowry with her," said Lady Lucas, "am not I right, Mrs Bennet? For Edward will inherit everything, will he not?"

"Yes, yes, I suppose so," said Mrs Bennet, who could not see where this conversation could go. "But Miranda will be provided for handsomely, I have little doubt."

34

"Pemberley is in entail to Master Darcy," said Lady Lucas, with an insistence alarming to both her hearers. "And the estates in Wales and Yorkshire will go to him – and all the treasures and the carriages and jewels, am I not correct, Mrs Bennet?"

"Mama," said Charlotte rising, "it is a hot day and we are all fatigued! Mr Collins will be most put out, if we are not back at Longbourn before noon . . ."

"Then it is just as well," closed in Lady Lucas, in a manner that was by now highly disagreeable to her audience, "that Master Darcy makes himself aware, even at his young age, of the pitfalls and pleasures of life in the capital. He may then avoid them when he comes into his inheritance. It is to be highly recommended."

"What is this?" cried Mrs Bennet, who mopped her face in the heat, and called for a dish of tea for her visitors, in the hope that her visible apprehension could be explained away by the sudden realisation of being remiss as a hostess. "I cannot offer apologies more sincere than I do now, my dear Charlotte – and dear Lady Lucas . . ."

"It is imperative we go, Mama," said Charlotte – but now there came the sound of Mr Collins outside, and his bluff greeting of the butler in the hall; and Charlotte sighed.

"Mr Collins is so anxious to have you back at Longbourn that he comes himself to escort you there!" cried Mrs Bennet, but to no avail; for that gentleman, bowing to Mrs Bennet, soon explained that his motive for walking over to Meryton Lodge had in no way been connected with the planting of his kitchen garden, or with the speedy reinstatement of his wife and mother-in-law at home.

"I was working in my study, Mrs Bennet – if I may so describe the room your dearly departed husband liked to think of as his library – "

"It *was* his library," said Mrs Bennet, in a sharp tone of voice.

" – when I saw a most interesting equipage – I cannot imagine that it came from Meryton Lodge, if it had not been for the stable lad, who ran behind and informed me you had

35

indeed received such a visitor. I cannot say, dear Madam, that the coach was all Lady Catherine would recommend, in appointment and magnificence – but there is not much to choose between that coach and her very own carriage, at Rosings!"

"It was not Lady Catherine de Bourgh, however," said Lady Lucas, in a voice intended to be cunning. "It is a personage new to this locality – a personage from London, I dare say!"

Now Mrs Bennet chose to simper, and to distract herself with the tea things, lately brought in.

"Whoever it may be," said Mr Collins, while Lady Lucas glared at him for his inept manner of tackling so delicate a subject, "it is the property of a family who knows how to maintain a fine household!"

Charlotte, thinking of the rooms at Longbourn where she could sit separate from Mr Collins, rose, announcing she feared for the head-cold of her youngest child. She would go back through the park unaccompanied, if needs be.

"If it is someone important from London, it is possible they bring news of young Master Darcy," said Lady Lucas, for her time, as she sensed, was running out. "Sir William tells me he has seen your esteemed grandson, Mrs Bennet – in Piccadilly!"

"Whoever may be the occupant of so splendid a carriage," said Mr Collins, who seemed unaware of the exceedingly unpleasant effect of this news on Mrs Bennet, "he or she will not die intestate, as will poor Sir William. It cannot be counted, the number of times my dear father-in-law has been advised to make his last will and testament. Yet his life at court has bemused him; he sees only his own immortality, when in the vicinity, however far removed, of the monarch; and he leaves a wife and daughter hideously unprotected!"

"Mr Collins, please!" said Lady Lucas, who was horrified at the lengths to which her son-in-law would go, to obtain the information he desired from Mrs Bennet. "Sir William's affairs are his own, if you will recall!"

Charlotte, who had grown very pale, now walked to the

door; and her abrupt departure went some way to bring the company to its senses, on this very warm day.

"I shall go with her," cried Lady Lucas – for offence at the indiscretion of Mr Collins was now the only option left to her. "I offer sincere apologies, Madam . . ." And, rising to her feet with some degree of difficulty, Lady Lucas inclined her head stiffly.

"Yes, yes, we must take our leave," said Mr Collins – "indeed, I was surprised to find you at Meryton Lodge at all, Mrs Bennet! For you must prepare for the happy day of the nuptials of Lady Catherine's nephew, Colonel Fitzwilliam, at Pemberley, must you not? I am astonished that you are not among the guests who toast the union of Colonel Fitzwilliam and Lady Sophia!"

Mrs Bennet replied that Colonel Fitzwilliam was not her family; this must be known to Mr Collins, she supposed.

"He is Mr Darcy's cousin," said Mr Collins, in a tone so odious to Mrs Bennet that she looked in vain for sympathy to her friend, Lady Lucas. "And I now learn that Master Darcy will be at the marriage. It is his exeat from Eton, and Mr Darcy has granted him leave. Lady Catherine writes to tell me so." Here Mr Collins, who appeared as oblivious to the relief of Mrs Bennet at this news as he had been unaware of her earlier agitation, made a show of assisting Lady Lucas into the hall; and it was not long before Charlotte was joined by her husband and mother on her walk back through the park to Longbourn.

Mrs Bennet permitted herself a triumphant smile, as her guests finally departed. Mr Collins had brought her the truth of Edward's whereabouts, exposing Lady Lucas as little more than a mischief-maker. Further, the party had gone home without the knowledge they had come to seek. Although Mrs Bennet had a desire, which was near irrepressible, to confide the name and station of her recent visitor, only Mrs Long would do as confidante – and, once the figures of Mr Collins and Lady Lucas had been swallowed up in a heat haze on the road to Longbourn, Mrs Bennet ordered her carriage and went upstairs to prepare for an excursion to the town.

Seven

Mrs Long had not experienced the splendid carriage in Mrs Bennet's drive, and was at first too distracted by her own affairs to pay much attention to her visitor. "There is the card table to be got to the menders! How can I put up a card table for Major Merriman and Miss Merriman this evening if the legs are to buckle as they did last week?" demanded Mrs Long. "I was promised a man all of three days ago, who would see to it, but he did not come! They say there is a bad influenza going about – though I find this hard to believe, in such a glorious summer as this!"

"It is glorious indeed," said Mrs Bennet, with an artful smile.

"It will have to be a musical evening," said Mrs Long, "and I never knew anyone play as badly as poor Miss Merriman – with the exception of your dear daughter Mary, God rest her soul! She has no idea of how to render a piece – I cannot put off the evening altogether, I suppose, for the lack of a card table – but I would, dear Mrs Bennet, if only I could!"

Mrs Bennet maintained a silence; and, as this was unusual in the extreme for her, Mrs Long soon offered apologies for her lack of delicacy, in talking of the late Mary Roper in terms that were disparaging and unkind.

"I cannot think what came over me, I really cannot! You must grieve so deeply for Mrs Roper – for your dear Mary, who, after all, stood in line to be chatelaine of Pemberley – if, that is, your daughter Elizabeth had not produced a fine heir for Mr Darcy!" Here Mrs Long stopped again; for she knew she was on dangerous ground; and that Mrs Bennet had not come into Meryton to discuss her grandson after so many years of anxiety on the subject. Remorse – for Mrs Long had a warm heart and did not like to see her friend suffer so plainly – led, after initial hints on the part of Mrs Bennet, to a series of outright questions on the nature of her visitor earlier in the day.

Mrs Bennet, however, now appeared determined to have Mrs Long wait for answers to her polite enquiries. "It seems I am entitled to a coat of arms – the very same as those emblazoned on the coach," said Mrs Bennet, by way of introduction. "They will do well for next summer, when I go with my granddaughter Miranda to court – indeed, I shall have them embossed on my writing-paper directly, for it does no harm to let the tradesmen at Meryton know exactly who it is they have been serving, all this time!"

"If your coat of arms will summon a table-mender, emblazon them now!" said Mrs Long, but with a laugh that was a little too hearty.

"I cannot truthfully say this new state of affairs will alter my position in the country," Mrs Bennet said, after a pause for reflection, which Mrs Long did not now like to interrupt. "I am invited to the eight best families in Hertfordshire as it is, Mrs Long. I was able to inform the Bingleys and Mr Darcy of this on the very first occasion of my acquaintance with them, at Netherfield. No, my standing in the country will not be changed, even if I must be addressed in another manner than that to which my friends have become accustomed!"

"And how must you be addressed?" asked Mrs Long, who now began to be alarmed. "You do not again intend to remarry, Mrs Bennet, I trust?"

Here Mrs Long restrained herself from referring to the unfortunate union, proposed by a Colonel Kitchiner of Uplyme, which had been about to take place shortly after the marriage of Jane and Elizabeth to Mr Bingley and Mr Darcy. "You would not wish to repeat mistakes of the past, Mrs Bennet," Mrs Long now found herself unable to resist remarking none the less.

Mrs Bennet coloured at the mention of Colonel Kitchiner – who had, as all Meryton recalled so well, been a fake and impostor, transpiring to be no more a colonel than a wet fish salesman – which, in point of fact, he was found to be, with a stall on the pier at Uplyme and a small house inherited from a wife who had died in suspicious circumstances.

"At my age!" Mrs Bennet protested feebly. "Forgive me if I say that I believe the destruction of your card table has put you in an excessively ill humour, Mrs Long; this cannot be the day to inform you of my discovery of a descent so momentous as to alter for me – and, I trust, for my dear daughters – all future prospects in life!"

Mrs Long saw that Mrs Bennet had become excited beyond a reasonable limit, and went to open the window. With some reluctance, she offered a peach sorbet intended for her evening party, which Mrs Bennet accepted and quickly consumed. "Your descent," said Mrs Long, pretending not to look into the glass dessert dish and its empty bottom. "What can that be, my dear Mrs Bennet?"

Mrs Bennet explained, in a voice so low in its modesty at first that Mrs Long had to strain forward to catch her words, that Lady Harcourt had come to pay a call on her this day at Meryton Lodge. Lady Harcourt had informed Mrs Bennet that they were related – that Mrs Bennet could, as much as Lady Harcourt herself, trace her ancestry to King William the Conqueror; and that she was as Norman as any Harcourt and had the right to use the name – if preceding her own, naturally – and the Harcourt coat of arms.

"Mrs Harcourt-Bennet," essayed Mrs Long. "It will take me some time to grow accustomed to it, I must own."

"You will grow used to it in a short while," replied Mrs Bennet sharply. "And you will kindly inform those of my acquaintance whom you may meet in town today!"

Mrs Long said she had no design to meet anyone other than the table-mender.

"Lady Harcourt invites me to London, and I depart shortly," said Mrs Bennet, who had been saving this important information to the last. "She has a house in Green Park – quite magnificent, it is said."

"Then it is probable that you will see your grandson,

41

Master Darcy," said Mrs Long, in a ruminative tone of voice. "Did not I hear from Lady Lucas that the young heir to Pemberley had lately been seen walking – or loitering, it may have been – close by? Was he not seen in Piccadilly?"

Eight

Elizabeth greeted her guests with the poise and sweetness for which she was known by all who met her; and she was happy to see that the gruff expression of admiration from Lady Catherine de Bourgh at the arrangements at Pemberley had a sincerity unmistakable in one who was so well used to speaking her mind on all subjects, however delicate.

"My dear Elizabeth, we must all be proud of you today. The house has seldom shown results of attention and respect such as yours – the shades of Pemberley are satisfied indeed!"

Elizabeth replied that a house so elegant needed no more than the deference its proportions demanded – though she was unable to conceal a smile at the recollection of the insolence, disapproval and disagreeability of Mr Darcy's aunt at the time of his marriage to a Miss Elizabeth Bennet. That she must take credit for the improvements at Pemberley she could accept; but Lady Catherine had, by a stroke of misfortune, been present at the time of Edward's rebellion and refusal to honour his parents – and she had not been pleasant on that occasion, either.

Elizabeth's high spirits never deserted her for long, and she put these memories aside; for was not the formidable Lady Catherine de Bourgh at her most amenable now? And did not this much improve the prospects for a harmonious midsummer meeting at Pemberley? There was, Elizabeth had to confess, her own great happiness to be considered as well – for was she not happier today a hundred times than she had been nineteen years ago? And were not she and Darcy more in love than ever? To go alone with him to the city

43

in the sea, when the nuptial celebrations were done, could be seen as a second celebration of her own marriage to Darcy – and Elizabeth knew his feelings were akin to hers. Lady Catherine must sense the connubial delight, Elizabeth thought, between her nephew and his wife – and she must, for all her determination to prevent the match at first, be now reconciled to it. Then the intelligence that Edward, after such a difficult start, now proved himself worthy of the family name, had also to be a strong factor in Lady Catherine's changed demeanour. Elizabeth was delighted to answer her enquiries on the nature of Edward's progress at school, as well as the type of conveyance chosen to bring him to Derbyshire and the route selected by his father for the purpose.

"He should be here by four o'clock and will dine with us," said Elizabeth. "Edward is certain to be as overjoyed by the happiness of Colonel Fitzwilliam as we are – for he was set on a sporting life, and Colonel Fitzwilliam instructed him in every aspect of shooting, fishing and hunting. That Mr Falk has remained here, to help him continue with his studies in the holidays, has rounded his education off perfectly."

"It is a pity he cannot add some inches to his height," said Lady Catherine. "I do not believe there has been a master of Pemberley of such small stature, in all its history!"

Elizabeth was vexed by this, but resolved to pay little heed to Lady Catherine – though she had minutes earlier complimented her silently on her improved attitude to her nephew's family. "Lady Sophia comes sooner," said Elizabeth, thinking it best to change the topic away from the shortness of poor Edward; "I dare say you have already made her acquaintance, aunt Catherine?"

"Certainly not," came the reply. "It is not a habit of mine, to roam about in the wilds of Scotland. One never knows what savage one might encounter there."

Miranda came into the long gallery, where her mother entertained her great-aunt, and placed two bowls of yellow roses on tables about the room. She was aware of Lady Catherine's quizzical stare – but, like her mother, was more inclined to disregard the manners of Lady Catherine than find herself distressed by them. Today, however, she was unable to prevent herself from making her own amusement, at her aunt's expense, and asked, in an innocuous tone instantly recognisable to Elizabeth, whether Lady Catherine knew anything of the home from which Colonel Fitzwilliam's bride came today.

"A castle a great deal larger than Pemberley!" said Miranda, who refused to meet her mother's eye. "Very old – the home of Macbeth, so Colonel Fitzwilliam was informed."

"What nonsense, Miranda!" said Lady Catherine, as the girl looked away to hide her laughter. "These tribes know nothing of civilisation, they fight among themselves, and erect piles of stones they call castles!"

Mr Darcy now came into the room, smiling, and with Colonel Fitzwilliam to one side of him and Colonel Fitzwilliam's bride on the other. Miranda, receiving a reproving glance from her mother – for Elizabeth was convulsed at Lady Catherine's portrayal of the race from which her nephew's bride was descended, and could only appear to frown, to conceal her mirth – now ran up to greet the pair; and in this way they were brought to meet Mrs Darcy and Lady Catherine de Bourgh.

Nine

Lady Sophia Farquhar was a slight, erect woman, with eyes that were deep set in her face and hair that was not fashionably dressed – she might be taken for a boy, who had grown up without receiving the necessary intelligence of her gender – or a woman, at least, who wished to make clear her abnegation of female vanity. That there was nothing superficial about her was soon made clear when Elizabeth, pressing the hand of her new cousin most warmly, wished her every happiness in her future life.

"Marriage is an act of choice," replied Lady Sophia, in a voice that was both hard and loud, so that Elizabeth wondered that Colonel Fitzwilliam could bear the prospect of passing a lifetime within earshot of it.

"Indeed," said Lady Catherine, who came closer to inspect her nephew's bride; and a note of approval could be detected in her tone: "I dare say you know what you have chosen. A man on an army pension does not live in castles. However well he may do with his sheep and livestock, he has no choice but to cut his coat according to his cloth."

"Such is the fate of a second son," said Colonel Fitzwilliam, smiling; and Elizabeth recalled, with some annoyance at her old friend, that he had complained of his poverty as the second son of an earl when she had first made his acquaintance, at Rosings, and that she had chided him for it, as they walked in Lady Catherine's very large park.

"I shall be a farmer's wife," said Lady Sophia. "I shall be as the housewife in the Bible."

A voice now came from behind the new couple; and the

47

company was able to perceive that Mr Falk, Edward's tutor, had joined the assembled guests and family.

"There is no housewife in the Bible," said Mr Falk.

Elizabeth contained her merriment – and made introductions. Mr Falk, naturally, was known to Lady Catherine; he was tolerated, barely, by Mr Darcy; and Miranda was thoroughly attached to the old man, whose bald, domed head and increasingly irritable utterances formed a good part of the fond memories of her childhood. Whether his manners, in correcting Lady Sophia on her knowledge of Holy Writ – and therefore of her own future role as the wife of Colonel Fitzwilliam – could be condoned, was, however, questionable, and Elizabeth resolved to speak to Mr Falk later, gently, on the subject of his greeting of the new guest of honour at Pemberley.

"I wish you to come and see the chapel, and approve its decoration," said Elizabeth to Lady Sophia. "I expect there are additional touches you would like, and we would welcome them – for Miranda and I have worked to our own specifications and need your advice."

That Elizabeth had learned tact and diplomacy in her years as the wife of Mr Darcy was acknowledged and appreciated far and wide. None of this could prevent the next arrival in the long gallery being seen as unwelcome in the extreme – and for a moment Mrs Fitzwilliam Darcy of Pemberley evinced the sensations of bewilderment and apprehension she had known at her first party of assembled guests, shortly after her marriage. She felt her colour go up; and felt also Lady Sophia's eyes, which were as dark and round as pebbles, staring at her curiously.

Miss Caroline Bingley – for it was she who had come in now, succeeded by her brother Charles and Elizabeth's adored sister Jane – had never married. After her hopes of securing Mr Darcy as a husband were dashed, she became more and more fastidious in her choices of escort; and within a few years ended up alone, grateful – it was to be supposed, for gratitude was never expressed – to receive a dower house on Charles Bingley's small estate. As aunt to

Jane and Charles's children she had shown herself far from perfect: her propensity to find the dark and unpleasant side of life led her to tell tales which frightened the young Bingleys exceedingly; and it was as much as the good-natured Jane could do to prevent her brood from knowing aunt Caroline as a witch.

Caroline Bingley greeted Lady Sophia with a stare as frank and fearless as that of the future spouse of Colonel Fitzwilliam; and, while Elizabeth suffered within at the possible reasons why her old friend – and Darcy's cousin – should elect to marry a person such as Lady Sophia, she had also inwardly to admit Miss Caroline Bingley might finally have met her match. She had not counted, however, on Miss Bingley's opening remarks – and was angered even further to discover her own reaction, which was distinctly one of annoyance, probably due to a building of tension – tension she was normally well equipped to disperse. "I do wish, dear Lizzy, that you would tell the herdsman at your model dairy to take care not to pull the horns from the poor bulls with such ferocity! To come down the road into the beauty of the park at Pemberley past the screams of those wretched animals is enough to turn the stomach, entirely!"

"It is not necessary to inflict pain on the beasts, when performing such an operation," said Lady Sophia, in a voice that sounded now like a trumpet, or a foghorn at sea in the night. "There are modern methods, in the rearing of livestock, both in shearing a bull of its horns, and in removing its testicles."

Even Miss Bingley now appeared to regret her choice of subject; and started to ask of Lady Sophia's family and its possessions.

"I have heard tell many times that the Farquhar collection is the best north of the Border! That your mother, the countess, has been delightfully portrayed by Allan Ramsay; that at Castle Farquhar there are Italian masterpieces to equal none in the country; and that a great library was built up, which is the envy of the finest in the land. You will return there frequently with your husband, no doubt – "

49

"If it is the lambing season I shall certainly not travel," said Lady Sophia in a tone that seemed to admonish everyone in the room for neglecting their duties to their herds and flocks. "I shall be up at dawn, to light fires and griddle pancakes for the shepherds; I do not expect to have much time to go north of the Border; and, in any case, a cousin inherits who is practically a stranger to me."

"This is the devilry of entailment," Lady Catherine burst out. "Why must a place be entailed in the male line? As Sir Lewis made sure, our daughter Anne inherits Rosings, and there's an end to it!"

"It is not courteous to our guests, to linger too long on the subject of entailment," said Mr Darcy – who smiled, to show his welcome of his cousin's bride, but was clearly about to lose his patience. "May I suggest that we go to inspect the work of Elizabeth and Miranda in the chapel? And the day is fine – we may take a walk in the park, for thunder is threatened later."

"Oh no, Papa! We cannot have thunder!" cried Miranda, who went to hang on his arm, and whose evident affection for her father soon improved the atmosphere among those gathered to meet the bride of Colonel Fitzwilliam.

"Why in heaven's name is he marrying *her*?" Miss Bingley said in a loud whisper, as the party went down through various halls and flights of wide stairs, to the chapel. "I cannot understand it at all!"

"Nobody ever did anything very foolish except from some strong principle," said Mr Falk, as they all hung back to allow Lady Sophia entrance to the bedecked and scented private chapel at Pemberley.

Ten

Elizabeth was grateful that Jane was a guest at Pemberley, and could be found, after the quick tour of the chapel and its decorations, in her room, washing mud from the face of her young son, and talking to her eldest daughter, Emily. The girl, who was nineteen now, had been one of her aunt's favourites since she was a small child – a time when Elizabeth had gone over to Barlow often with the troubles of her early marriage, to ask advice of her sister and Mr Bingley. "It is strange that such a quantity of dirt should be found, on a beautiful midsummer day," said Jane, laughing, "but the lad has been playing at the farm, doubtless – and tells me he was given work to do at the dairy."

Elizabeth's mortification at Miss Bingley's portrayal of the agony of the animals now came irresistibly out; and, when she had done, Jane shook her head gravely and dispatched her son to the nurseries, where a bowl of fresh berries awaited him, and a game of shuttlecock afterwards, in the park, with his brother and sister. Emily, also, sensing her mother wanted to be alone with her sister, made an excuse and left the room – but not before passing by Elizabeth and planting a light kiss on her cheek.

"You should not heed Lady Sophia, Aunt," said the girl, in a grave tone that was pleasantly tempered with wit; "for she has ideas of her own, and wishes to impose them on others – why, before she was even upstairs to meet you, she was in the kitchens dictating the nursery meals. 'No blancmanges,' she said, 'but fresh curds done the Scottish way, strained through muslin and eaten with no adornments whatever.'" Emily spoke in the loud voice

51

of Lady Sophia, and both her mother and aunt burst out laughing.

"How does she think she may go to the kitchens without my permission?" cried Elizabeth; then, seeing Jane's expression, she laughed again, and shrugged the matter away.

"She did not like the display Miranda and I set up in the chapel," said Elizabeth, "for she says buttercups and daisies are God's flowers, yellow and white and from the fields, unlike the lilies and white roses we have cultivated here at Pemberley – devil's garlands, I dare say she thinks them."

"It is odd, when by all accounts her family is so far from being coarse and unpolished, that they are known everywhere for their taste, refinement and wealth," said Jane. "Lady Sophia has lost her castle to a cousin, and makes amends for it with her severity of outlook, perhaps that lies at the root of it."

"But Miranda will not inherit Pemberley – she is the elder of the children and she might rightfully feel a sorrow about it. She loves the estate, she understands the farm – yet not once has she complained that Edward has it all, when the time comes!"

"Miranda has few to equal her," said Jane quietly. "Lizzy, you are sad, I see, to lose a friend in Colonel Fitzwilliam, for you cannot believe a friendship can be sustained with his new wife. It is sad – but, in a year or two, each will have found an interest which precludes unwanted meetings; and you will have Colonel Fitzwilliam as a friend to you and Darcy in just the same measure as before!"

"Why, Jane, though, why?" cried Elizabeth, for she could see no solace in a future happiness so long postponed. "What can he see in her? Lady Sophia is just the reverse of the woman dear Colonel Fitzwilliam might be expected to choose, as bride – "

"He needs help with his livestock," said Jane. "He needs a partner, for farming on land that is mostly moor and inhospitable to profit and a luxurious way of life!"

"You are right," said Elizabeth, her head drooping, "I

forget that we are rich, and Colonel Fitzwilliam must make such living as he can, from poor land. No – Lady Sophia is an ideal farmer's wife."

Jane and Elizabeth looked away from each other here, to avoid giving vent to their mirth; but to refrain from further comment was impossible for Jane, who went on to say, in a gentle tone, that Colonel Fitzwilliam had for so long been in love with Elizabeth as to make it difficult to see the virtues in any new bride.

"You know it is true, Lizzy. He has worshipped you – since before Darcy's proposal at Rosings! He has lived only for your happiness – and to ensure that Edward will be a fine sportsman, and keep away from trouble, as he grows older. You fear the loss of him – and it is for Darcy to take a greater measure of care, in the matter of rearing children! For, though it is plain to see his love for Miranda, he has never had the patience of time a child such as Edward requires and deserves – and all have suffered because of it. Indeed, I see that you dread the absence of Colonel Fitzwilliam, in this respect – but you must permit the man his own life, his own happiness!"

"You are right, Jane!" said Elizabeth. "I have grown so selfish, I can scarcely believe it of myself. And I do know", she added quietly, "that Darcy is not at ease with children. Why, our very first Christmas here, he let me feel that – though he had a good reason to stop the children's party, where I had put so much effort and care!"

"It was a good reason, indeed," said Jane, whose sense of justice and sweetness of nature had grown since her adoption of Charles Bingley's son, and her acceptance of this secret in the past life of her husband. "But, whereas Charles will build the lives of his children, with words and tree-houses and anything they may need, Darcy adheres to principles of a bygone age. His father was more tender, in his rearing of Darcy and his sister, than the present master of Pemberley! But you love him still, Lizzy – and it is only to be hoped that you will prevail on him, now he has relented to the degree of allowing Edward here for the wedding, to speak to his son as an equal, and to approve his actions rather than condemn him for them. I do not wonder that you miss Colonel Fitzwilliam as mediator between father and son."

"I shall try," said Elizabeth – and she then confided to her sister that she and Darcy would have the opportunity to talk of Edward when they were in Italy together, and away from Pemberley. "For here, I confess," said Elizabeth, "there is so much the question of inheritance, that Darcy's every judgement of his son is clouded by it. To be far from Mr Falk, with his own views of the progress of Edward, will also make it possible for us to see with clarity – I promise you, Jane!"

Steps here sounded in the passage, and the sisters moved apart, for they had come to resemble conspirators, seated near each other by the window.

"I shall try to believe you, Lizzy," said Jane, smiling, "but I see a pair of lovebirds in Venice, rather than conferring parents, I confess!"

Elizabeth smiled and shook her head, as the steps came to a halt by the door, and Darcy's voice enquired of Jane if her sister were within.

Jane replied that she was; and could be seen smiling all the more when Elizabeth went out of the room to him, and low voices were heard. The voices were followed by happy laughter, and by a rustle of silk, as Elizabeth, led by Mr Darcy, swept along to the apartments of the master and mistress of Pemberley.

Eleven

The days had become unconscionably stretched out for Mrs Bennet at Meryton Lodge; the nights were the shortest of the year; and the absence of any invitation to leave Hertfordshire was galling in the extreme.

"I cannot see why you do not go to Kitty, for a change of air," said Mr Collins – for he was the recipient of many calls at this time, intended for his wife Charlotte, who had the habit of finding urgent matters to attend to when Mrs Bennet was announced at Longbourn. "Kitty is always glad to have you, even if the social circle she inhabits is of a restricted nature, with few members of any distinction. Brighton is not far off; you may make excursions there, Mrs Bennet!"

"Mrs Harcourt-Bennet," Mrs Bennet reminded him in a grim tone. "Do not forget my new style, Mr Collins, I do ask of you."

"Mrs Harcourt-Bennet," said Mr Collins, with a sneer not so well disguised as he imagined. "If your friend Lady Harcourt invites you to London, why do you delay in going there?"

Mrs Bennet said no day had been fixed – "and I have so much to see to here, Mr Collins! The Lodge must be painted inside and out. The roof must have a new guttering. I am most dissatisfied with the state of the garden. A place cannot be allowed to run down – especially when the proprietor and kind benefactor will shortly visit!"

Mr Collins expressed himself astonished by Mrs Bennet's assertion that she would receive so rare a visitor as Mr Darcy at Meryton Lodge.

"A letter came this morning – from dear Elizabeth! She

understands very well that we may not have the amenities to which Mr Darcy is undoubtedly accustomed. She suggests a visit shortly after the marriage at Pemberley of Colonel Fitzwilliam and Lady Sophia – for the Darcys go to Italy, directly after. I am most disappointed, Mr Collins, that they have not chosen Sanditon or Weymouth. I hope I may suggest to Mr Darcy that he build a seaside villa down there. It would be most salubrious for the children, and I would be invited there, to chaperone dear Miranda, I have no doubt of it at all!"

"Lady Catherine advises strongly against the coastal regions," said Mr Collins, "for the air is most harmful to the lungs, and the persons who spill out on the beaches of the bigger towns are reprehensible in the extreme!"

Charlotte Collins here came in from the garden, carrying a basket of fruit. For all her good nature, she had begun to dread Mrs Bennet's visits; and, as she had that morning also been the recipient of a letter from her dear friend Elizabeth at Pemberley, she found herself glad to learn that Elizabeth and Darcy would visit Meryton, on their way to the Continent. That it was a long time since Elizabeth had seen her mother was painfully acknowledged; and with the acknowledgement came expressions of guilt. "Darcy kindly accepts the idea," Elizabeth's letter to Charlotte had gone on, "and he claims he will be happy to revisit Netherfield – where we first made acquaintance, as you well know." Elizabeth signed off by wishing her dear Charlotte all the happiness in the world, and a good level of impatience until they should meet again; and it was a measure of this delightful impatience, very probably, which caused Charlotte to express a sharpness with the mother of her absent friend, which she would not normally have permitted herself. The presence of Mr Collins, who was brought by these visits from rooms where he could in the usual run of things safely be expected to stay all day, was doubtless another factor, in Charlotte's brief greeting of Mrs Bennet. Whatever the cause, a walk round the garden was soon decided against, and the offer of Mrs Collins's pony and cart quickly accepted.

"I am only sad," said Mrs Bennet, as she climbed into the conveyance, "that we have not had time enough to talk, dear Charlotte! I had brought some scraps of cloth to show you – some fine brocade, some silk organza, and a sprigged muslin I am informed by Mrs Long is a great deal too young for my years!"

Charlotte replied that there would be time to see the swatches when Mrs Bennet came again – and, delightfully, in the company of Lizzy.

"I hope, at least, that one of the dresses I have sent for will be ready by the time Mr Darcy comes to Meryton. A fine dress, Charlotte – how much you have missed, in my telling you of it! – embroidered with gold thread and pearls!"

Both Mr and Mrs Collins assured Mrs Bennet of their impatience to see the dress.

"Lady Harcourt has it made for me in London," said Mrs Bennet, as she put up her parasol, and the driver urged the pony to move on, for it was a hot day.

"Lady Harcourt?" said Mr and Mrs Collins, in a rare unison.

"The dress will do very well for Miranda's presentation at court, so it will serve well for several occasions. I have dispatched to her fifty guineas, and this does not include the subscriptions I send to her charities, my dear Charlotte. For to be a Harcourt is to be generous to the poor!"

Before Charlotte could exclaim at the sum of money extorted by Lady Harcourt, Mr Collins had turned on his heel and gone into his study – where there was an imposing volume, dedicated to satisfying the curiosity of any who wished to learn the lineage, and all other relevant information, on such as Lady Harcourt.

"It looks very strange, Charlotte," Mr Collins said, at all subsequent occasions of his seeing his wife, in dining-room or parlour at Longbourn. "It looks very strange indeed."

Twelve

Elizabeth could not recollect a time, since her first year at Pemberley, when she had viewed with such keen apprehension the dinner which awaited the assembled party, at four o'clock. There was Mr Falk to look out for: it was true, as Mr Darcy said, from time to time in perfect good humour, that the aged tutor now saw himself as a preceptor; for, before the company went into the dining-parlour, he ventured various opinions to Lady Catherine de Bourgh which were not in the least well received. The most disturbing of his pronouncements had come when Miss Bingley, reluctant though she might be to acknowledge a good happening in a family, had offered the congratulations of her sister Mrs Hurst and herself on the occasion of Master Darcy's recognition of distinction at Eton.

"Master Darcy's success will make you sought after, Mr Falk! Elizabeth and Darcy will be sorry to lose you here, I dare say."

To Elizabeth's consternation, Mr Falk had said roundly that he would eat his hat if his pupil had gained any kind of distinction – and Lady Catherine had glared at him all the more when he went further, to say it was more probable that one of the cellar-boys in the kitchens of Pemberley would gain such a distinction than Master Darcy; and the boy must have invented it all by himself.

"This is most alarming," announced Lady Catherine, who fixed her gaze on the old man to no good effect, for he seemed unmoved by her attentions. "Do you hear, Darcy? We have a case of false pretences here, or so Mr Falk believes."

Elizabeth saved her husband this time, from Mr Falk's

increasing cynicism and indifference – but she had reason to dread the meal ahead, which was designed to celebrate the arrival of the bride, Lady Sophia, and could therefore be expected to be of some hours' duration. She could only conclude that Darcy had been kind, when he said Mr Falk should not leave Pemberley – yet Elizabeth, even if she would own it to no one but herself, feared that Darcy also knew that Edward might need the tutor again one day. Then – which she could not own, either – a large portion of Mr Falk's remarks seemed true to her. She had woken several times in the night since the arrival of Edward's letter, wondering that there had been no confirmation of his success from the school; but Darcy appeared satisfied with his son's method of conveying the good news – and had gone so far as to comment on the much-improved nature of Edward's hand, which was now impeccable indeed. And Darcy had shown understanding, in the question of Edward's trip north for the marriage of Colonel Fitzwilliam. To feed him with further suspicions on the nature of his son would have been far from diplomatic.

The day was fine, and Elizabeth decided to go out walking before the dinner hour. She had taken Lady Sophia to her room, and now felt herself a Midas, or at the least a frivolous and pretentious woman of little taste, after hearing Lady Sophia's barbed comments on the Chinese wallpaper and magnificent flowers. She would go high up on the hill, to the Hunting Tower – and look out over other counties, where each family might have its trouble, but at least it was not hers to fret over. She would sit in the look-out place where the lonely Queen, Mary Stuart, had sat and watched the horsemen riding to hounds, sounding out in the valley below her. It could be enchanted as a midsummer day could make it – and, if Elizabeth had a premonition that she would not be the sole admirer of the beauties of the landscape, this was once more something she kept buried deep inside her.

It was in all probability a growing fear that Edward had not spoken the whole truth, or that he might not come after all today, which – when put together with the presence of Miss

60

Caroline Bingley under her roof at Pemberley, and Lady Sophia, another challenge it was hard to meet – led Elizabeth to run the last stretch of woodland path to the summit of the hill that overlooked the surrounding countryside. She did not look back, as she was accustomed to do, and smile down with a pride and a sense of accomplishment, however modest, at the park, with her new cascade, the ornamental lake, and in the distance the roof of her model dairy. Today, she looked ahead; and had to conceal a smile at the earnest look of anticipation in the eyes of Mr Gresham, who stood up there also, surveying in his case a part of woodland where once he had felled trees and widened paths for the Darcys and their relations to walk along and better enjoy the view.

Elizabeth admired Gresham's success as an architect in London. After a successful career at Oxford he had risen without difficulty in his chosen profession – for Gresham would never occasion doubts as to his skills and prowess. As Elizabeth had on many occasions sadly conceded, there was no Edward Darcy in him, only ability and hard work and an ambition tempered by charm. Now, so it was said, he had designs to become a Member of Parliament in these parts – and it was also said that his Radical and progressive views were much praised in the locality, by forward-thinking landowners and estate workers alike. Elizabeth liked to see his stance, on this high point above Pemberley; and did now concede, without bitterness, that Mr Gresham could easily be taken for lord and master of the estate. She did not care for Darcy any the less, and knew he admired her for keeping a warm place in her heart for the bailiff's son – who had been so generously educated and supported by her husband; and who had assisted her selflessly at her time of uncertainty. She felt something of an affinity with him – a brother, as she could see him, though she knew, certainly, that Mr Gresham had much to do to encourage brotherly feelings for her in return.

The wind blew, in exquisite shafts of light air; they were high up enough to hear the lark sing over the green hills beyond the confines of the estate; and Gresham, allowing the freedom of the place to overtake him, came down the path to Elizabeth, and stopped in his tracks. She looked up at him, and it seemed to her that the day grew longer still; and that the dinner need never take place, where Mr Falk would annoy Mr Darcy, and Miss Bingley would annoy everyone else – while Lady Sophia, doubtless disgusted with the fine repast her hostess had taken so long to design with the housekeeper, Mrs Reynolds, might, for all she cared, call for bread and milk.

"You will feel the lack of your old friend when he marries tomorrow," said Gresham as he came up closer, "and I bring you all the reassurances in the world, dear Mrs Darcy, that I am here when you may need me. For when I go to London, I dream of you here; and when I am here I dream we are together in London – though I know this never can be!"

Elizabeth felt her cheeks burn – but she was uncomfortably aware that her eyes sparkled as well and that she did not draw back from Gresham, who was so close to her now that she could feel herself in his arms, protected from the ill-assorted company at the house below.

"I go to Italy with Mr Darcy after the marriage," said Elizabeth; and she thought herself a flirt as she uttered the words, but could do nothing to improve matters. "On the route, we break off and visit my mother, in Meryton. So I do not think I will visit London in the foreseeable future. But I do wish you well, in your campaign here – "

"You will come – and hear me speak in Chesterfield?" said Gresham eagerly.

Elizabeth shook her head, but found, to her intense shame, that when Gresham came close to her she did not pull back. Only a distant bell – and Elizabeth knew it to be the old clock on the tower at Pemberley, its chimes borne up through the woods by the wind – told her she must run down the path – and that, run as she might, she would be late.

"I have come too far, and I have stayed too long," was all she could say to Gresham – who made no move to stop her now, but stood back, his eyes following her, as she flew down the path.

How she could have passed such a quantity of time, when it seemed she had only walked up to the Hunting Tower and exchanged a word with a friend, was a mystery to her. She could only believe, at a later hour, that some prophetic impulse had sent her in search of freedom for the very last time – before returning to news which must alter her life for ever.

Mr Darcy stood in the hall, his face pale and a letter in his hand. Elizabeth saw, as in the wild patterns of a dream, that Lady Catherine stood by his side – and Lady Sophia and Miss Bingley together by the foot of the stairs. Colonel Fitzwilliam was there as well – and this, if anything, assured Elizabeth that the faces she saw before her, with their dreadful expressions, showed more than simple concern for a dinner hour missed; for Colonel Fitzwilliam was not prone to go in to eat without the presence of the hostess. He knew her love of walking alone; the absence of Elizabeth would have given him the opportunity to inform the guests there was no cause for anxiety; yet his face showed only shock and grief.

"Edward does not come to Derbyshire," said Mr Darcy, when his wife reached his side and looked up at him, full of apprehension.

"He has overturned his carriage!" cried Elizabeth, who had feared this a hundred times.

"He has gambled away the Welsh estates," said Darcy in a voice so clear and cutting she could swear she had never in all her years with him heard it in employ. "He had a tick at a gaming house in London; he has fallen into the hands of moneylenders; and I must go to London directly."

"Moneylenders?" cried Elizabeth, who now saw her sister Jane approach, and went to take her arm, half fainting. "Will they harm him, then?"

Darcy, still in this different voice, said curtly there was no question of Master Darcy's being harmed. He would go straight to London, and see what repairs could be made in so perilous a situation. So saying, he strode from the house; Elizabeth saw his horse was already there for him; and she groaned at the thought that her dalliance in the clearing in

63

the wooded hills behind Pemberley might cost her husband or her son his life.

"Come, Lizzy," said the practical Jane, as she led her sister to the stairs, and upwards to her room. "All will be well. Let us at least be thankful that Mama is not here today!"

Elizabeth smiled a little, at this; but she was unable to prevent herself from hearing Lady Catherine's comment as she went up the stairs, leaning on Jane's arm, that Edward's wrongdoing was "all down to bad blood"; or Miss Bingley's, that "ill management by the mother" was the root and cause of the crimes and misdemeanours of young Edward Darcy. Fortunately, Lady Sophia's strictures on the successful rearing of livestock, and the lessons to be learned and applied to a Black Sheep in the family, were lost in the domed ceiling of the hall; and Mr Falk shuffled in from the dining-parlour too late to pass any judgement on the latest performance of his charge.

Part Two

Thirteen

Elizabeth had much to contend with in the days that succeeded Darcy's terrible announcement, and his abrupt departure for London.

She had first to continue with the preparations for the festivities at Pemberley. Mr Darcy had extracted a promise from Colonel Fitzwilliam that, come what may, the marriage would proceed as planned; and there were details to be attended to, which were far from Elizabeth's liking, at that time. Musicians, with their ideas for jigs and wedding marches, seemed quite out of tune in the sombre surroundings that all of a sudden had become her home. A swan of spun sugar, with a flotilla of confectionery boats and tugs, was to be set up as the *grosse pièce* of the table, in the banqueting-room at Pemberley; but the frivolity appeared outstanding to Elizabeth; and she went for relief to the darkness of the shuttered State Bedchamber, seldom used by the master and mistress of Pemberley, for it suited her mood more, at this time, than shafts of summer sunlight and artificial, sweet absurdities set up on the long table.

The weather, as if to mock the prospects for the future of this great house and estate, was so perfect that it could be said to resemble a stage set for a fairy-tale, a midsummer night's dream. It was a windless day; the sky was as enamel blue as the boxes and *objets de vertu* kept on the tables of the newly opened drawing-rooms, and was set, as they were, in gold, for the sun was as bright and hot as it had ever been known at Pemberley. The topiary yews, so carefully designed by Darcy and Elizabeth together in days that seemed already to belong to a distant age, shone bright on their chessboard of moss and grass, the king's crown and queen's sloping figure unchanging in their squares, as the sun shifted angle and showed them up against the façade of the house; and their very lack of motion served only to stress the sudden alterations that took place at Pemberley.

Elizabeth left the State Room, with its great fourposter, and walked down stairs and landings to Edward's room. As she went, she reflected, with a sadness she had never known, that Darcy could not reign for ever; he must grow old and die; and Elizabeth must stand down, one day, and leave this place she had tended and loved over all these years. This was the autumn, come when she least expected it, at the height of summer when the village at Pemberley danced and rejoiced. There would be no future now, for Pemberley.

She was in Edward's room when from the window she saw a carriage approach through the park; and for the first time since the destruction of all her hopes and happiness there was consolation at least – for here came aunt and uncle Gardiner, guests at the wedding, and as yet unaware of the disaster that had befallen their niece and her family. For a minute or two, at the sight of their happy faces as they alighted by the bridge – at uncle Gardiner's request, certainly, for he would spare no time in searching for trout or grayling, darting under the bank in clear water – Elizabeth could believe the events of the past hours had been nothing more terrible than a dream. But, turning back to the room inhabited by Edward in the holidays from school, and seeing his pencil portrait executed by a visiting artist many years ago that showed his slight features and childish smile, she knew all was changed now and never could be restored to the old certainties. A box of soldiers, tidied by a maid, but still protruding at an angle from his shelf of toys, brought a tear to Elizabeth's eye – until her sense of reality, her spirit, which could not be quashed for long, reasserted itself, with the truth of the past and the present coming together in an urgent need to plan, to survive somehow, the shock of all that had gone wrong.

There had been, from the start, something angry, rebellious

– Elizabeth could not employ the word "bad", even to herself – in the boy. The soldiers – all Bonaparte's men, some broken and with paint peeled with the battles set up by Master Darcy against the men of England, the dragoons he called the Pemberley Brigade – stood for his early refusal of his place in the hierarchy here. She had known, perhaps, from those early years, that Edward would disgrace himself, and, with himself, the name of Darcy – and that he would lose all that would rightfully have been his. But the knowledge came near to destroying her; and her courage faltered once more, so that she wished only to conceal herself – or to take comfort with Jane – to disappear, rather than break the news to the only relations on her side of the family invited to the marriage at Pemberley. She felt the shame of the recent discovery that her son was a disgrace; but she knew that, if Darcy came to disown him, she never could. Edward was her flesh and blood – even if he brought down the line of his forebears and was expunged from it, so future generations would not know he ever had been born, or lived.

Such a fate, for the son greeted with love and welcomed with relief, by both his mother and father at the time of his birth, was almost too much to bear; and Elizabeth thought she heard the bells of his christening peal out, as she went down to greet her aunt and uncle. The bells were practice for the wedding – she could immediately understand – but the gleeful sound was almost intolerable to her. Edward was lost – with all the land and tenancies and smallholdings and valleys and villages he had diced away – and there might as well be another bell tolling for him, one that was muffled, and severe and sad.

Fourteen

Elizabeth had become aware, over the years at Pemberley, that social niceties must be kept up, whatever the weather; she was looked to, by now, to preserve calm and decorum, at times when others might exhibit panic or show emotions too fully for comfort; yet it was with difficulty that aunt and uncle Gardiner were taken to make the acquaintance of the future bride, Lady Sophia, and harder still to find so little time for the breaking of the bad news before footmen swept them up into the long gallery and thence to the library, where the company was at present assembled.

The Gardiners, in turn, wore solemn expressions, and tried to show a gaiety commensurate with the occasion – but with little success, for they were honest, decent people unused to pretence. Lady Sophia, once the introductions were effected, made it at least possible for Elizabeth's relations to frown in earnest, for her diatribe against the methods in which children were brought up nowadays could hardly fail to induce a degree of apprehension in the hearer.

"No one in my family was kept at home, from the age of one day! A wet-nurse was found in the village; the child, if a boy, was sent early to school – there would be no question of keeping a healthy fellow at home, with a tutor!"

Lady Sophia directed a baleful glance at Mr Falk, as she spoke; and the other guests, who stood about in stricken attitudes, some partly hidden by the splendid bookshelves and columns of the library, now came in close and took seats on sofas and chairs. Refreshment was brought and Elizabeth had no choice but to act the hostess, to the full; but her inclination, as she handed a glass of lemon water to Lady Sophia,

71

was to drop it down her dress and to show no repentance of the act afterwards.

"Edward had a good head for numbers," said Mr Falk.

Lady Catherine de Bourgh here emitted a sound, a har-rumph, that had Caroline Bingley convulsed with mirth, and Jane indignant and distressed, as she showed by a painfully heightened colour and look in the direction of Elizabeth.

"A good enough head for numbers to lead the young scamp to drain his cup and place in there something still more pernicious, namely a pair of dice!" said Lady Catherine. "He has lost fifty thousand pounds, by gambling away Brecon and the outlying farms. My sister, Lady Anne Darcy, loved Wales and would be devastated to hear of this loss, for when she was alive, as mistress of Pemberley, she would go there as often as possible. She was much loved there, as a benefactress to those who worked on the land. Not a rick was burned in Lady Anne's time! It is sad to consider that this lack of interest in Wales, as demonstrated by his mother, has led Master Darcy to show his contempt, and lose the estate entirely!"

Elizabeth was made angry by this, and remarked in a quiet tone that her ties with Brecon and the Welsh estates were known, in the locality – but she could not deny, as she had silently to admit to herself, that there had indeed been years when her anxieties over Edward, at home with his tutor at Pemberley, had caused her to dissuade Mr Darcy from their annual visit.

"Is it not a fact that Master Darcy is under age, and his debts can have no validity, under the law?" enquired Mr Gardiner.

"My dear Mr Gardiner," replied Lady Catherine, "the boy has fallen into the hands of moneylenders! They will exact their payment from my poor nephew, you may rest assured. The foolish fellow has frequented gambling-houses and billiard-hells; he has plunged with delight into the game of hazard, and has obtained a tick at a hotel in Covent Garden, where he drinks pale ale in the mornings and develops a fine career in theatres and singing-houses,

72

beating the town at night. It is here that Mr Darcy should go looking for him!"

A silence ensued after Lady Catherine's declamation, in which every member of the party wondered at the surprising acquaintanceship with debauchery of her ladyship; then a buzz of talk broke out, as Colonel Fitzwilliam came into the library, with an announcement, in turn, to make.

"I only wonder that an elaborate scheme of education, such as was provided here by a special tutor," said Lady Catherine, who was not to be so easily silenced, "can have produced such dire results. Logic, moral philosophy and metaphysics, was it not, Mr Falk? The lessons in moral philosophy appear to have been particularly unsuccessful!"

"Nothing improves on discipline!" said Lady Sophia.

"I wish only to say", said Colonel Fitzwilliam, before Mr Falk could defend himself, "that I have been in consultation with my betrothed – and that both Lady Sophia and I are of the opinion that this is not an auspicious time for a marriage to take place." Here Colonel Fitzwilliam darted an anguished glance at Elizabeth, who felt for a moment his old love for her returning and blushed furiously, despite herself.

Colonel Fitzwilliam continued for some time to protest his desire to postpone the marriage – and so obdurate was he, that Caroline Bingley was heard to mutter that it sounded as if a cancellation was uppermost in Colonel Fitzwilliam's mind, and she did not wonder at it. It was for Elizabeth to calm, soothe and reassure: the wedding must take place, as arranged – had not Mr Darcy secured a promise from his cousin, before he left? – there were the guests to think of, many of whom would already have undertaken the journey – and so on and so on. In the end, Colonel Fitzwilliam assented; and further chaos was averted.

"If only to spare Mr and Mrs Darcy the expense of a ruined party, succeeded at a later date by a wedding planned anew, I must also give my agreement to the marriage going ahead," said Lady Sophia, when all eyes turned to her. "As a thrifty housewife, I do not consent to the spectacle of a pile of uneaten delicacies, and bottles of champagne opened that were never necessary at all!"

Elizabeth bit her lip at this – for to find herself accused now of extravagance in her stewardship of the kitchens and cellars at Pemberley was clearly but a precursor to the suggestion that Edward inherited his gambling streak and other nefarious habits from her.

"We intend to keep a tight ship," said Lady Sophia, in as loud a voice as had probably ever been encountered in the library. "Colonel Fitzwilliam and I have made together an estimate, to the last penny, of our expenses for the coming year. We will live exactly within our income."

Colonel Fitzwilliam nodded his concordance at this; but Elizabeth detected an air of unease.

"If you make an estimate of your expenses for the coming year," said Mr Falk across the room to Colonel Fitzwilliam, "and upon that estimate you find that they exactly amount to or fall a little short of your income, you may be sure that you are an embarrassed, if not a ruined man."

There seemed little reason in the company staying together after this, and Lady Catherine was the first to rise, saying she was going in search of Mrs Reynolds's nephew, who was an excellent piano-tuner; for her daughter Lady Anne came tomorrow, and had often found the instrument in need of adjustment.

Fifteen

Mrs Bennet had not been at home more than a day, since her last visit to Longbourn, before she found time hang heavy on her hands; and, not unusually for her, regretting the absence of a daughter at home in whom she could confide. Mary, whose marriage to Thomas Roper had taken her first to a tall, narrow house in Richmond – where Mr Roper followed his trade, as disappointed heir to Pemberley, of auctioneer at a house specialising in antique urns and stoneware generally – had, at her death, not been much missed by anyone, for she was silent, morose and concerned chiefly with her own bookish interests. Now, however, Mrs Bennet recalled only the days when, after the marriages of Jane and Elizabeth, and the going away of Kitty, not to mention the premature elopement of Lydia, there had been only Mary at home. She had been drawn out then, and encouraged to sit with Mrs Bennet and listen to her for hours on end. Her engagement, after their visit to Pemberley, had been a triumph for the mother, but had deprived Mrs Bennet yet again of a resident daughter; and as she found the summer evenings unbearably long, and crowded with memories that were not necessarily all pleasant, Lydia was sent for, on the grounds that Mrs Bennet was far from well, and in need of constant care and attention.

This was not the first time that Lydia Wickham had been summoned in this fashion; and it was understood between them that something of a beneficial nature would befall them both, in the event of her collusion. Lydia was burdened with children, and tired of trying to manage on Wickham's small pay, in a living near Lyme, at Pymore, a poor district where little notice was taken of the extreme unsuitability of her husband as a parson. She was desperate to come to Hertfordshire, which seemed now to be the acme of sophistication; and, on this occasion, Mrs Bennet had hinted at the possibility of a trip to London. Attempts to wheedle money from Mrs Darcy, her sister, had for many years been unsuccessful – despite Mr Darcy's legendary generosity to his poor relations – for Wickham, each time he was assisted with his income, went drinking or gambling; and, by now, even Lydia was shame-faced about asking her sisters, though Jane Bingley was still liable to be approached and asked for help. Only Mrs Bennet, who had a soft spot for her youngest and silliest daughter, was prepared to divest herself of funds – in return for company, sympathy and agreement in every respect, a matter not difficult for Lydia, who much resembled her.

Mrs Bennet was labouring over a letter to her daughter Elizabeth at Pemberley, when carriage wheels could be heard outside and the maid came in to say an invitation had come for Mrs Bennet.

"An invitation?" said Mrs Bennet. "Do go and see who it is from, Leah. I cannot say I expect an invitation at all, unless it is for poor Lydia, to await her arrival, and I am sure an invitation is just what she could most do with just now!"

Mrs Bennet having thus expressed herself, the possibility of days ahead without Lydia became apparent to her, and she hoped very earnestly that no invitation had come for her daughter. Footsteps outside brought the maid into the room once more – and the carriage wheels could be heard to drive off, before Mrs Bennet had time to open the thick manila envelope which was handed to her.

At this moment, a knock at the door brought Mrs Long, for a visit; and Mrs Bennet was quite flustered at so many things happening at once, on a day so utterly devoid of events only a short time before.

"I saw a splendid carriage in your driveway," said Mrs Long; "and as I was passing, to pay a call on Mrs Collins, I thought

I had better look in and see that all was well here, my dear Mrs Bennet!"

Mrs Bennet replied that she could see no reason why all should not be well at Meryton Lodge. "Mr Darcy's allowance is more than adequate, Mrs Long, for a poor widow like myself! And I have the arrival of Lydia to look forward to – all is very well, indeed!"

"It seems your invitation to the wedding has arrived very late," said Mrs Long, who now had her eyes fixed on the envelope. "Does not Colonel Fitzwilliam wed his Lady Sophia within a few days, if not less?" And Mrs Long went on to bemoan the delays in the express, in the area, and to recount the many funerals, marriages and the like cruelly missed as a result of this.

"I do not go to Pemberley," said Mrs Bennet with as much dignity as she could muster. A glance at the written message on the packet now brought a colour to her cheeks, however; and after a short pause Mrs Bennet felt at liberty to pass the invitation to her friend. "You will see to whom the missive is addressed, Mrs Long!"

Mrs Long made a fidget of finding her lorgnettes in her bag – but finally had no choice but to read out the name of the addressee and the words "Meryton Lodge", written just over a magnificent seal, depicting a coronet and a coat of arms.

"'Mrs Harcourt-Bennet'," declaimed Mrs Long. "Gracious, dear Mrs Bennet, shall I open it?"

"If it pleases you," said Mrs Bennet, with a studied casualness which in no way deceived her visitor.

"It is an invitation," said Mrs Long, after what seemed to Mrs Bennet to be as great a length of time as all the empty day that had just gone before. "An invitation to a wedding. A kinsman of Lady Harcourt – so she says, and a charming young girl, of the best possible family! At St James's' Piccadilly – "

"Enough, Mrs Long," said Mrs Bennet, rising and taking the letter with an air of brisk decisiveness. "I shall write directly, to refuse Lady Harcourt's kind invitation. Allow me, Mrs Long . . ." And Mrs Bennet bustled to the escritoire as if there were no time to lose in turning down so delectable an opportunity to visit London.

"But why in heaven's name do you not accept?" cried Mrs Long, as her friend had anticipated she would.

"I have my daughter Mrs Wickham here on that date," said Mrs Bennet. "I am not of the type who leaves their friends or relations in the lurch, when a better invitation comes, Mrs Long, as you should know."

"Take Lydia with you," urged Mrs Long. "If Lady Harcourt is to you what – let us say – Colonel Fitzwilliam is to Mr Darcy, it would be as improbable of Lady Harcourt to refuse an invitation to her kinswoman Mrs Wickham, as it would be of Mr Darcy to refuse permission for the marriage to take place at Pemberley."

Mrs Bennet frowned, since her lack of an invitation to the marriage at Pemberley was, as she well knew, a hotly debated subject at present in the vicinity.

"Come, Mrs Bennet!" said Mrs Long, as Mrs Bennet crossed already to her writing-desk and picked up her quill, intent on following her friend's advice without further hesitation. "You may well see other relations of yours there, you know; and your daughter and son-in-law may be glad of intelligence from you on the whereabouts of young Edward Darcy!"

For all Mrs Bennet's protestations that Master Darcy, if he was anywhere other than school, would most certainly be with his mother and father in Derbyshire, Mrs Long continued, in the gentlest of tones, to insist that Sir William Lucas had told her he had caught sight of Mrs Bennet's grandson in London very recently. "And, Mrs Bennet, by strange coincidence indeed, in Piccadilly!"

Sixteen

The day of Colonel Fitzwilliam's marriage dawned fine; a blue sky above the wooded hills of Pemberley showed Elizabeth, as she lay sleepless in her bed from the first breaking of the sun's rays, that her arrangements for eating alfresco in the water gardens would go undisturbed by water descending from above; and the cooing and calling of doves as they wheeled in pairs around the roof of the great house could be seen as further presage of a successful ceremony – portending possibly even undisturbed matrimonial harmony to come.

Elizabeth doubted this, but was too honest to deny her own feelings in the matter of Colonel Fitzwilliam's betrothal. She had counted on him too much – that was it. In the times of Darcy's sudden coldness – or absence, overseeing far-lying estates. He had become more than an equerry, sometimes, in her mind, a substitute for a husband who was by no means easy to accommodate or love without a strong element of faith. That he had Darcy's first name, Fitzwilliam, had been comforting, too much so; and he had taken the problems of Edward without a murmur of complaint; had civilised the boy, as his father had not had the patience to do; and, in teaching young Master Darcy the ways of the country, had demonstrated that a humane approach to beasts and the surroundings in which they lived was as good a way of coming into the world of grown men and women, when the time came, as any. Now he would be gone, from all their lives – and it was at this point, in the hundred times these thoughts circled in Elizabeth's head, that she drew herself up and clutched her head in her hands, before falling back on the pillow. For "all their lives" no longer had meaning now, for herself and Darcy and their son. Their lives were broken into fragments, and could never be pieced together again.

However much Elizabeth tried to stray from self-reproach in the matter of her behaviour over the past days, she was unable to resist laying the blame for it all – for Edward's defection, for Darcy's unprecedented rage, at the sight of her, for their strained marriage and bad example in the locality as successful parents – on her own vanity and propensity to indulgence of her desires and appetites. Had she not been jealous of Colonel Fitzwilliam's new-found happiness with another? Had she not been offended by the plain-spokenness and disagreeability of Lady Sophia, comparing her unfavourably to herself, yet all the while wishing for a more potent rival, in looks and charm, than the one poor Colonel Fitzwilliam had brought her? Had she not, in the fear of repudiation – which her years with Darcy had bred in her, for when he turned, in one of his incomprehensible moods, away from her, she knew herself exiled from life, from his heart, and from Pemberley – had she not allowed herself solace with yet another admirer, once Colonel Fitzwilliam no longer wooed her with painful restraint and fidelity? She had – and the thought of the hour in the woods, on the hills that rose soft and rounded, to show themselves in a perfect curve from her wide bed as she lay helpless in the toils of self-recrimination – caused blushes to rise to her cheeks that would have brought all but her husband to their knees. She had compensated for the loss of Colonel Fitzwilliam by the encouragement of Mr Gresham – she had raised Gresham's hopes, there could be no doubting that. And she had been as transparent on her return, to Mr Darcy, as any woman who has lived day and night in a close and usually ecstatically happy marriage can be to her husband, when she has betrayed him with another. Darcy had ridden off with a black heart, indeed – and the more Elizabeth considered it, the more her spirit failed her. He went in search of a son who had disgraced his name and lost his fortune. He left behind him an unfaithful wife.

Elizabeth was more unhappy than she cared to admit, when a light tap at the door brought her sister Jane, also admitting she had been unable to sleep – for it was so light and bright outside, and the grounds from the window so empty, apart from the cries of the birds, that she owned she had found it eerie, as if the wedding of Colonel Fitzwilliam and Lady Sophia had already taken place, and all the guests gone home, along with the newly wedded couple. Sensing her sister's wretchedness, she perched on the end of the fourposter bed and tied back a curtain that hung loose to its pole. Elizabeth smiled at this, but found herself near to tears: that Jane, with her neat habits, should be here with her, and not Darcy, who let the curtains around the bed fall down each night, so he might love Elizabeth with all the privacy they could both desire, seemed all at once to her to be a symbol of the future, and it saddened her beyond words to think of it. Jane she adored; Jane she could visit at Barlow, to her heart's content, and admire without envy the gentle manners and tall, well-formed son with whom Jane and Charles Bingley had been blessed, as second child after the delightful Emily. Jane she could count on for ever; but it could not be enough. She had thrown away her happiness – even her secret denial of Edward, when Miranda suggested to her that the boy should go with them to Wales later in the summer, had been yet another crime, in this series of disasters and disgraces that had fallen on the family.

"What nonsense, Lizzy!" Jane, hearing this sad litany, was as calm and reassuring as Elizabeth had known she would be. "It is something so commonplace, a boy going astray at this time of his life – and Darcy will bring the rogues who took advantage of his innocence to justice. You heard him say so, Eliza!"

Elizabeth confessed her secret guilt – but she did not go as far as owning to the feelings she had allowed Mr Gresham – for Jane, who was so liberal in her understanding and compassion of all human failings, was nevertheless a loyal wife, and would not comprehend the sudden sense of entrapment Elizabeth had suffered, at the prospect of the wedding party; and her brief desire to know the freedom of succumbing to the charms of Mr Gresham.

"Lady Catherine is out of countenance, now that Lady Sophia goes even further," said Jane, to change the subject entirely; and both sisters were soon laughing at the competition between the two terrible ladies, in their attitude to those they considered inferior in rank and importance. The question of why Colonel Fitzwilliam would choose Lady Sophia as his bride was as much avoided as any mention of other suitors of the lovely Mrs Darcy, in the woods at Pemberley or elsewhere; and soon Elizabeth was able to imagine her life restored to her, within a matter of days: Edward forgiven and repentant; the Welsh estates reclaimed; and Darcy beside her where Jane sat lovingly, smiling at her. All would be well; and soon, when Colonel Fitzwilliam came without his wife to Pemberley for dinner, they would talk and play billiards together as if no rift had ever taken place between any of them.

"We should not be so grateful at the absence of Mama, at this occasion," said Jane, who reproached herself, Elizabeth knew, as much as she did for the paucity of invitations to come north to Derbyshire or Barlow. "But, at a time like this, I cannot imagine the situation improving with her here at Pemberley."

Elizabeth agreed, and added that she had written to Mrs Bennet, emphasising that she was to be a guest at Christmas this year, and was even to come as early as the first of December, to make sure the roads were still passable and not made hazardous by snow.

"That is very good of you, Lizzy," said Jane. "I suppose she will come."

"Why should she not come?" enquired Elizabeth, whose thoughts, she was sorry to confess, were once more with Darcy; for her eyes were led astray by a fine Canaletto over the fireplace at the end of her bedchamber, which showed the Grand Canal at Venice – and from there she dreamt of Italy, and the sea, in the weeks they had wished to spend together, now so much in jeopardy.

82

"Mama has a new friend, who claims to be a cousin of ours," said Jane, frowning. "I could fetch the letter, but it would wake Charles. This woman's name is Lady Harcourt, if I recall. Mama has sent her ten guineas, for some charitable cause, and thinks she will visit her in London, I believe."

Elizabeth was puzzled by this, but not much concerned – she had many other matters to think of and the arrangements for the day to attend to – for time with Jane passed rapidly, and the sun rose at last in the sky above the windows of Pemberley.

Seventeen

Lydia arrived promptly at Meryton Lodge, this unaccustomed punctuality being attributed, by Mrs Bennet at least, to the fact that the possibility of a visit to London was hardly worth the posture of fashionable lateness.

Mr and Mrs Collins had extracted the promise of a brief visit, before Mrs Bennet and her daughter left for the capital; and on this occasion Lady Lucas's husband, Sir William, was to make a rare appearance – for, as was well known in the vicinity, Sir William had come to prefer the Court of St James to the comforts of his own home and the company of his family. He had information to impart, so Mrs Bennet was told – and she was not reassured to hear it – and Mr Collins also had the fruits of his research to share with the good lady at Longbourn.

"My dear Mrs Bennet," said Mr Collins as soon as Mrs Bennet and Lydia had stepped from the carriage, "I have a most remarkable thing to show you ..." And here he bustled them to the garden, behind the house, while Charlotte could be seen looking with surprise at the guests led so suddenly to the greenhouses.

"I do not know which to tell you of first!" cried Mr Collins, who appeared agitated today beyond the normal expectations of a fine summer's day and the prospect of a neighbourly visit, followed by a dish of tea. "Both are monumental!"

"We cannot stop long," said Lydia in a cross voice. "We have business in London – at least I do, Mr Collins. Some may enjoy their incomes, in private; others, such as Mr Wickham and myself, have no choice but to earn our livings."

Mr Collins replied that he was aware of Mr Wickham's

living at Pymore, but had been unaware of his wife's entry into the mercantile classes. "Lady Catherine de Bourgh will have nothing to do with tradespeople, you know," he said in a voice that was intended to terrify, as if from the pulpit; "she will not speak with progressives or liberals, either: she will have things as they were set out to be, by the good Lord."

"She is right, I am sure," said Mrs Bennet, who became each minute more nervous.

"I am in the business of buying and selling objects of virtue, carpets, tables, and the like," said Lydia, who now adopted a lofty tone, to counterbalance Mr Collins. "I am an expert in my field, Mr Collins; and, while Mama enjoys herself with Lady Harcourt, I shall be occupied with providing a good income for my children and my poor husband, for the coming year."

"Lady Harcourt – yes . . ." said Mr Collins, throwing open the greenhouse door and ushering in his guests. "I have had to keep her under glass the last month or so, to await the dry weather; now I believe we have a fine spell assured for the rest of the month, I shall bed her out – and invite the village to judge she is the biggest in the locality!"

"What can you mean, Mr Collins?" cried Mrs Bennet, who saw, to her relief, a small party consisting of Charlotte Collins and her parents Sir William and Lady Lucas leave the house and walk across the lawn towards them.

"My apologies!" beamed Mr Collins. "I have so much to tell you, Mrs Bennet, that just now I spoke of my prize marrow and not of your new benefactress. I have had recourse to a volume in the library Mr Bennet left us here – and I have gleaned some excellent information for you, therein. Lady Harcourt is a woman of immense fortune – with a fine house in Kent – not as grand as Rosings, I will say – but definitely in a category which would merit an occasional call from Lady Catherine herself!"

"Goodness," said Mrs Bennet, as Lydia grew thoughtful at the quantity of bibelots, fine tapestries and china Lady Harcourt must possess. "And how about London? We go to London to visit her, Mr Collins, not Kent."

"Yes, she has a house adjacent to Devonshire House, no less," said Mr Collins, "at Green Park. Now for the treasure of Longbourn – beyond price, would you not concur, Mrs Wickham?" And with a smirk of satisfaction he pulled a glass cover from a long bed of earth on a trestle table, and revealed a marrow that was indeed impressively large.

"Aha, so you are tending your vegetables, Mr Collins," said Sir William, who had just now entered the glasshouse, preceded by Charlotte Collins and Lady Lucas. He spoke in the jocose tone of an urban man who makes a rare excursion to call on a country bumpkin. "And how goes it, if I may enquire?"

Lydia yawned in a very ill-mannered way. "Mama, the carriage waits, and it grows oppressively hot," said she. "Can we go to London, I beg you!"

"I am most delighted to know", said Mr Collins, frowning, but unable to resist picking up the marrow and holding it aloft, "that we, too, my dearest Charlotte, may claim kinship with Lady Harcourt! I informed our daughter Amy as soon as my researches were done; and I believe she has been overwhelmed by the knowledge, and keeps quiet on the subject, when we meet!"

"Lady Harcourt is not known to me," said Sir William, who was as pompous as a man almost always to be found at the court of St James feels the need to be, when addressing such as Mrs Bennet. "But the Dowager Duchess, who is now in her ninetieth year and with remarkable powers of recall still, was frequently a visitor, as a child, to Harcourt House. The paintings are very fine – by Titian and Tiepolo – and there is statuary in the courtyard. Most impressive, I assure you, Mrs Bennet!"

Mrs Bennet felt her importance rise greatly with Sir William, and with his son-in-law; she assured them she had been invited to give her approval to the marriage, which she and Lydia would attend, and had gladly done so; and she would have stood simpering a while longer, if Lydia had not escorted her to the carriage, and bade adieux for both of them. Mrs Bennet felt gratitude for the speed with which

Lydia organised their departure – for Lady Lucas had topics as yet unaired, and very little time to open them out, with the carriage wheels turning, and the horses pausing at the side of the road which would take them at last to London.

"Sir William tells me he was mistaken, when he thought he espied your grandson, Master Darcy, in London, Mrs Bennet!" Lady Lucas said into the coach window. "Is that not so, Sir William?"

"I was most certainly mistaken," puffed Sir William, walking alongside the carriage, which had now set off at a fast pace. "I was coming up St James's, y'know, and I could have sworn I saw the lad – but it was a long time since Mr and Mrs Darcy last came to Meryton – "

"I cannot spare the time to have my life filled with people all the year round," said Mrs Bennet, half leaning out of the window, but determined to make her point to Sir William. "It was a short-statured man I saw – and I was most certainly mistaken – for Master Darcy must be on the verge of manhood by now, a fine figure I have no doubt . . ."

Inside the carriage, Lydia tugged at Mrs Bennet's skirts and brought her back in.

"A man with a wife, and a baby in her arms! It is true, the first time I thought it was Master Darcy in Piccadilly, he was alone – it was he, I could swear to that – but this time – no, it is out of the question, naturally. Please accept my apologies for having alarmed you, my dear Mrs Bennet!"

The carriage now started to gather speed; but the pace of the horses did not deter Mr Collins, who ran abreast of the passengers, for the purpose of thrusting the marrow in at them, with instructions for its delivery to Lady Harcourt, in London.

"I cannot give as freely to charities as yourself, my dear Mrs Harcourt-Bennet," panted Mr Collins to Mrs Bennet and Mrs Wickham, who now found themselves each holding one end of the vegetable, "and Lady Catherine believes, rightly, indeed, that there are more undeserving poor than there are those to whom giving is justified! But Lady Harcourt may discover a worthy recipient of my most humble offering!"

Lydia enquired, now that they made good progress on the London road and Mr Collins's portly figure was left far behind, what on earth they would do with the marrow, once they and their equipage arrived at Harcourt House. "For if we leave it in the chaise, Mama, and it is espied by a footman, it will seem as odd as presenting it to Lady Harcourt, will it not?"

To this Mrs Bennet could give only the vaguest reply.

Eighteen

It was generally agreed, by newcomers, as well as guests of many years' standing, that Pemberley had never looked so splendid as it did today.

Tables to seat a hundred or more had been set up on the grassy swards by the water staircases; a cold collation, of fowl and fish from the farms and rivers of the Darcy estates, would be consumed to the sound of splashing water; and all this would be washed down with the finest champagnes and wines from the Pemberley cellars.

Pyramids of roses, tied together by McGregor the gardener and his workers, since dawn, stood as dividers of these outdoor banqueting-rooms – which were also marked out with box hedges, so the agreeable sensation of being "at home" while under the sky was reinforced. For good measure, Elizabeth had sewn canopies of a delicate sprigged muslin, to give the feast its proper hymenal air; and these billowed softly in the light breeze, above the tables where Colonel Fitzwilliam and his immediate friends and relations were to be seated. A gondola with a cargo of rose-petal sorbets awaited in the icehouse, to appear at the time of the toasts to the happy couple; this would be drawn by invisible strings along the stream that bordered the garden at Pemberley. Fireworks would be let off from the Palladian bridge. Murmurs of approval, at Elizabeth's exquisite taste and ingenuity, made a low buzz in the crowd; all was well at Pemberley, and no mention, in all that low hum of talk, was made of the absent master and his son and heir.

Elizabeth found herself the cynosure of all eyes, as she made her way through the assembly, greeting strangers, friends and acquaintances with the sweetness for which she was acclaimed everywhere. Those with liberal sympathies and kind hearts smiled at her long and concerned conversation with Mrs Wilberforce, who had lost her daughter only three weeks before; those of a worldly disposition approved Mrs Darcy's polite, quick tone when conversing with the ancient friends of Lady Catherine. Miranda, with her fine figure and dark eyes, was seen to be the exact likeness of her mother, and to have inherited her kind nature, for she, in turn, was a long time commiserating with the estate manager's wife, Mrs Gresham, on the recurring sickness which prevented old Mr Gresham from attending this important event.

There was sympathy and understanding in some quarters for the way in which Miranda had begged her father to let the old man stay as estate manager at Pemberley, when a sterner employer would have replaced him years ago; but there was also mention, among those who had heard a story from one with impeccable credentials, that Miss Darcy's fervid interest in the new agricultural methods and machinery, and her ability to twist old Mr Gresham round her finger, had been the motive behind her plea on the manager's behalf.

If people spoke of Mr Darcy – and some said he was too good to his cottagers, because of his wife's tender feelings for their circumstances, while others said Mr Darcy would never move with the times and had publicly refused to show interest in a new threshing-machine on an occasion when Colonel Fitzwilliam persuaded him to pay a visit to Chesterfield Fair – they spoke in the understanding that Mr Darcy himself would soon appear, and Master Darcy with him. The news had got about that young Edward was a worthy scion of the family, and many expressed a wish to set eyes on him, now he had attained sixteen years of age.

No one, apart from the close family, knew of the difficulties in which Elizabeth found herself. They saw a smiling face, to which they were happily accustomed; and they did not see the one face to whom this smile was not directed, or notice Mrs Darcy's colour come and go should she happen to find

herself in the vicinity of the bailiff's son. Young Mr Gresham
was considered handsome, that was all; there was even talk
of an understanding between the son of the estate manager
and Miss Miranda – but there was too little evidence, and
the rumour soon drifted away, under muslin canopies as
gossamer as an insect's wings.

Elizabeth felt the need for reassurance, at this first sight
of Mr Gresham since her ill-fated dalliance in the woods,
and she went in search of Jane, as she did on every occasion
when love, compassion and friendship were needed. It was
not easy, however, to reach her sister; and she soon found
herself waylaid by some, and overhearing the conversations
of others, none much to her liking, she had to confess.

"My dear Lizzy!" cried Miss Caroline Bingley, who
scoured the skies, from under the rim of her parasol, for
some evidence of a cloud that would come and mar the
happy occasion. "I do think it will rain! Mr Darcy said
there would be thunder, before he departed. Did you hear
anything of him, yet?"

Elizabeth replied, with a greater severity than she had
intended, that she had no news of Mr Darcy at all.

"I have heard that those who are seized for their debts
are thrown directly into prison," said Miss Bingley – who
now waved at her sister Mrs Hurst, as she entered one floral
room by the aperture in a box hedge only to vanish once more
from sight. "I saw that you spoke with Mrs Wilberforce,"
persisted Miss Bingley, but not until her talk of prison had
secured the anguished look she desired, as it flitted across
Elizabeth's face. "She has lost her daughter – and now she
may well lose another, in the coming week! Poor Flora has
a canker of the breast – you may imagine, dear Elizabeth,
the agony of the surgeon's knife, when the breast is removed
entirely!"

Elizabeth made her excuses and left Miss Bingley. Now it
was her duty above all to find the bride, and inform her that
the marriage in the chapel must commence. She could see
the parson, a tall man with an honest, open face – as unlike
Captain Wickham, who had once begged for the living at

Pemberley, as it was possible to imagine. This in turn led to secret feelings of gratitude, that Lydia and her family – and Kitty and hers, as well as Mrs Bennet, on this occasion – were all absent from Pemberley. Poor Mama, Elizabeth thought, as she made her way through the throng; if she had only made herself more serious, when she was young, her marriage might have been a happy one! That her life was quiet and settled, now; and that the generosity of Darcy had made this feasible for the widow, was nevertheless a great comfort to both her eldest daughters. Mrs Bennet's years, in old age, would be calm and comfortable, with her friends at Meryton. The vague memory of a new acquaintance for her mother, spoken of by Jane, brought a frown to Elizabeth's smiling face, as she tried to recall the particulars – but Lady Catherine, resplendent in wedding attire, now approached and laid an arm on Elizabeth; her daughter Miss de Bourgh stood beside her; and Lady Sophia, in a simple lawn smock, stood not a few feet away, a garland of field daisies around her brow.

"Lady Milhaven has yet to make your acquaintance, my dear niece," said Lady Catherine. Elizabeth knew, from her style of address, that Darcy's aunt, formidable though she might be, felt compassion for her today – and that she would ensure, also, that Miss Bingley and her sister were aware of the consequences of airing their views on the subject of Mr Darcy's absence, and the disgrace of his heir.

"I am delighted with Colonel Fitzwilliam's bride," said Lady Milhaven, a tall woman with small eyes that darted in every direction. "Living, as we do, on land that joins with the Matlock farm – I know how inhospitable the terrain can be. There is more loss than profit to be had; Lord Milhaven tells me he would prefer to be a laundryman in Manchester than attempt to squeeze a living from our rocks and stones! Lady Sophia will be economical indeed!"

Elizabeth agreed that Lady Sophia showed herself already to be prudent in the extreme; though the thought of Lord Milhaven, a local figure known for his rotundity and fondness for port, as a laundryman, had her wishing again for Jane, that they might enjoy the relief of laughter together.

"Lady Sophia informs me that she has visited the cottages on the Pemberley estate," said Lady Milhaven. "She is not fond of wasting her time, as so many women are these days, whether in lying about reading novels or the like."

"Indeed!" said Elizabeth, who felt a sense of indignation that Lady Sophia should have done any such thing. "I do not think the cottages at Pemberley are in the province of Lady Sophia's interests, Lady Milhaven! The cottagers are regularly visited; their complaints are heard; and both my daughter Miranda and I supply other needs, in our weekly distribution of food and medicines."

"Oh, Lady Sophia does not *give* to the wives of the men who work the estate, Mrs Darcy; she *takes*. This I thought you knew of, for it is clever indeed, to make riches from rags!"

Elizabeth was about to demand an explanation from her new acquaintance when Lady Sophia came towards them, her face showing a high colour, due to the increasing heat of the day.

"I am amazed at your modesty, Lady Sophia," cried Lady Milhaven. "Do tell Mrs Darcy of your visits to the cottagers at Pemberley!"

"I ask only for their rags," said Lady Sophia, in a strident voice which appeared to belie any claim to modesty. "I make up carpets with them, Mrs Darcy – indeed, I presented one to Lady Catherine, only today!"

Lady Catherine said the rug would do very well in the parlour at Rosings. But Jane, who had come up to find Elizabeth at just that moment, was able to take her sister by the arm and lead her to an enclosure in the high hedges of the garden, where the sisters could indulge their mirth to their hearts' content.

Nineteen

Elizabeth was not formed for ill humour; though her prospects of happiness might be destroyed, at least until news
of Edward came, she was soon able to make a voluntary
transition to the subject of her daughter's uncertainty on
the fortunes of her brother, and cease from thinking of
her own misery. Miranda was pale; and, in her attempt
to hide her anxiety from Mrs Darcy, unusually abrupt in
her manner; and it was with some difficulty that Elizabeth
persuaded her to accompany her to the chapel, where the
marriage was about to be consecrated. Miranda must fear
for her brother – she had the courage and high spirits of
her mother and would not say so, for fear of disturbing her
– and besides this, as Elizabeth had often admitted to Jane,
if to no one else, Miranda was her father's daughter and
favourite. She was a Darcy, in her abilities and expectation
of governance; her orders, when given, were issued with
lightness and wit, but demanded obedience, on the instant;
and, like Fitzwilliam Darcy, she avoided the tag of arrogance
through charm and thoughtfulness, always disarming when
apparently inconsiderate. Not least, as his senior by a year,
Miranda had shown Edward from infancy that she would
protect and assist him in every way; and Elizabeth detected,
as they walked at a gentle pace to the east door of Pemberley,
the air of a bird that has lost its young, in her daughter – for
without Edward she had no outlet for her strong feelings of
sisterly love; and no prospect of further occasions for the
sibling laughter Elizabeth still heard echo in the house on
the occasions of the boy's return from school.

Elizabeth had arrived at the point – useless, as she knew it was, even to contemplate – of wishing Miranda to be the one to come into the estate of Pemberley, if it could not be her son, when a bulky figure stopped Mrs Darcy and Miranda by the entrance to the chapel, and bowed low before them, thus obstructing their progress with a measure of ineptness that was at once recognisable to Elizabeth.

"My dear Mrs Darcy! Allow me to pay my addresses to yourself and to your very lovely daughter!"

The figure straightened up: Elizabeth saw that Miranda smiled, for the first time that day, and was glad she could feel still, even if ridicule was the sensation that came most immediately to mind. For Thomas Roper – Master Thomas Roper, as the young man had been called by all who suffered him, since his first visit to Pemberley eighteen years ago – could not survive an allusion by any member of the family without an accompanying smile, comprising both hilarity and pity. Roper was the man who, brought to Pemberley by Lady Catherine a year after Elizabeth's marriage to Darcy, had been introduced as next in line in the entail, should Elizabeth not provide an heir. The birth of Edward, coming, as it did, a year after the Darcys' daughter, had pushed him once more to the background. In the meantime, much to Mrs Bennet's delight, he had married Elizabeth's younger sister Mary; and Christmasses at Pemberley had from that time counted the couple as visitors. Since Mary's death, Elizabeth owned to herself that she had neglected to invite Thomas Roper. He was a distant cousin of her husband, that was all; and his company had been known to organise a large party of people to set out walking on the moors in the most unseasonal weather, rather than hear his monologues and soliloquies. That he came to the marriage of Colonel Fitzwilliam was not surprising, however: Lady Catherine as kinswoman would have seen to it that he attended. Colonel Fitzwilliam, as her nephew, was a relative of Thomas Roper; and none of the pleas that he be omitted – laughingly couched, it was true, by Elizabeth and Miranda to Mr Darcy – could be heard. Roper was here; and now, not content with his first greeting, he bowed low over the hand of Miranda, who stepped back sharply at the unwelcome attention.

"I am needed in Richmond, but it has been a matter of obligation to attend the marriage of my cousin Fitzwilliam," said Roper in low tones which indicated an increased degree of self-importance. "I work on my inventions, Miss Darcy; but I do not neglect the ideas and influences which come in from Egypt, the most ancient of civilisations. I see that all is at Pemberley as it might have been a century ago – even the nuptials, I dare say, will be conducted in a manner unchanged since the Reformation. Why cannot we follow the customs of a country so much more evolved than our own; why are there so many who resist the examples of Egypt?"

"Egypt?" said Elizabeth, for she saw Miranda had to look away to conceal a smile. At the same time, a crowd built up, to gain admission to the chapel; and Elizabeth recalled, with a good deal of annoyance, that Master Roper appeared incapable of understanding the needs – or, as at times she had considered in the past, the existence of the rest of the world. With a rapid gesture, she waved to Master Roper to stand aside and allow the guests admission to the chapel – but as he failed to take any notice of it, and Elizabeth succeeded only in pricking herself on the thorn of a rose-bush, no progress was made, and Mr Roper continued with his speech.

"I have drawn out the plan of a Great Pyramid, to be constructed in the centre of London, which will provide accommodation for five million corpses, my dear Mrs Darcy! The scheme will shortly be approved, so I am told, by the very highest levels of administration. Many villas are to be designed, which will show the Egyptian influence. Why should not our marriage ceremonies also be performed under Pharaonic law?"

"Why not, indeed?" said Elizabeth, who found her own reactions of mirth and sorrow at this occasion very nearly overwhelming – for was not her son lost, her husband gone in search of him and of a large portion of the family fortune? – and, as she had seen so many times in her life with the connections and descendants of the family into which she had wed, a strong element of farce appeared always to distract her from the most sombre of occasions.

"I have long wished to inform you of my multifarious projects," Thomas Roper now said – to Miranda alone, Elizabeth could not help from noticing. "My calculating machine, for example – a great deal faster and more efficient than the contraption of poor Mr Babbage!"

Miranda professed herself delighted to hear of Mr Roper's schemes; and, finding an opening in the crowd, which now poured round them on to the grass and made their way into the chapel, took hold of her mother's hand and went with a firm tread indoors, while Mr Roper was left to make his way as best he could. Music sounded out from the interior of the great house; women adjusted their bonnets and men removed their hats; and skirts and breeches and shoes scraped and rustled on the pews of the private chapel at Pemberley.

Twenty

Mrs Bennet and Lydia found all the discomforts of the journey vanished away, once their carriage turned into the Mall, with the fine prospect of St James's Palace ahead, and to the side of them a park where fashionably dressed men and women walked by a well-situated lake.

"I am unsurprised that Sir William Lucas spends all his time here," pronounced Mrs Bennet, as she watched a very fine gentleman indeed descend from his chaise and enter the portals of the Palace; and the sight of a bunch of young rakes, on their way to Regent Street and the gambling-hells and smoking-divans of Piccadilly, did nothing to dispel her good-humoured appraisal of the vicinity. "There is no one like this in Meryton," she assured Lydia – who assumed an air of fatigue, to show she had visited London many times before. "There are no arcades there, Lyddy – and Mrs Long in her new gown would look quite dismal! I prefer it to Bath – there is no comparison at all!"

Lydia remarked that they should look out for their destination and tell the driver, before they were caught up in a press of carriages going to some rout or other in Haymarket – "for we could be here for hours, Mama: we could find ourselves at an assembly where we were uninvited, all by mistake."

"We could find ourselves at an audience with the King!" cried Mrs Bennet. "And I very much doubt he would turn us away, Lydia! We came over with the Normans, you must recall what I have told you – it is hardly probable that a man from Hanover, or Holland, or wherever it may be, would refuse us entry to his gates!"

"Did not Lady Harcourt give directions as to how to find

her house?" enquired Lydia in a cross tone. "Is it not on the card, Mama?"

Mrs Bennet replied that Lady Harcourt had no need of anything so vulgar as an address; everyone of consequence knew where she lives – "adjacent to Devonshire House, no less, Lydia – and everyone knows that!"

Lydia asked in a tone that was even more snappish if the driver was to be considered a person of consequence – for, as she had predicted, the Bennet carriage was now caught in a swirl of sedans, chaises and phaetons, all ensnared between Piccadilly and Haymarket, and the chance of getting free seemed remote, indeed.

"The driver knows the way," was all Mrs Bennet would give out, though she spoke doubtfully, her eyes trained backwards out of the carriage, to the mansions which stood alone facing Green Park. "He is perhaps not permitted to go directly there," said Mrs Bennet, for in any situation hope was the last of the qualities to leave her. "We are not accustomed to all this commotion, Lydia – it may be we will have to go by another route in order to go back up there!"

Lydia shook her head in disagreement – but, before any further conversation could take place, the coach was jolted violently, as if someone had delivered a vicious kick to the horses, and Mrs Bennet's equipage had broken away from the line of waiting vehicles, to be carried at speed up Regent Street and beyond. A figure had mounted the box – this was all they could see – and the first relief at movement, on the part of the stationary carriage, was superseded by alarm.

"This cannot be right!" cried Mrs Bennet, who was thrown back on her seat and threatening palpitations. "Tell him, Lydia, for Heaven's sake – he goes the wrong route, and much too fast!"

Lydia's cries were of no avail, however, for the carriage rattled up the great curve of Regent Street and into an insalubrious quarter, where small, dark houses crowded against each other – and, apart from the odd party of young hell-raisers, there were only women on the street, all in a finery quite unlike that of the residents of St

James's, as espied by Mrs Bennet from her carriage window.

"What can they be thinking of, Lydia?" said Mrs Bennet to her daughter. "It is not becoming, to wear such colours and to sport so low a décolletage! I dare say Lady Harcourt does not permit such persons outside her house – she cannot live here, Lydia, she cannot be privy to all of this!"

As Mrs Bennet spoke, the carriage came to a halt, and a loud burst of swearing was heard from the coachman, as a bucket of steaming ordure was thrown into the narrow alley from an upper window, narrowly missing the driver but splashing the sides of the coach. A stunted man in the dress of a pageboy, with greasy livery coat and a pigtail, now wrenched open the door and held out a hand – in a white glove that had seen better days – to assist Mrs Bennet and Lydia into the street.

"Harcourt House?" said Mrs Bennet, in a voice that wavered. "We are invited to attend a marriage, by Lady Harcourt – "

The reply came that Lady Harcourt awaited Mrs Bennet and Mrs Wickham within. Before the coachman could make further enquiries, the man who had jumped on the box at Piccadilly was also down in the street, and aiding the pageboy with his escorting of Mrs Bennet and Lydia down an alley too narrow for a carriage to follow. Mrs Bennet and her daughter looked back once – but, as they were unable to remonstrate, the driver cracked his whip and made his way out of the maze of Berwick Street to the main thoroughfare in Soho. His instructions, from the party who had paid him handsomely to go to Hertfordshire and collect Mrs Bennet and Mrs Wickham, terminated with the deposit of these ladies in London. Before long, the carriage that had been the conveyor of Mrs Bennet on her important visit to the great city had been swallowed up once more in the crowd.

Twenty-one

Elizabeth seated herself in the chapel, with the uncomfortable sensation of being watched by a hundred eyes; and, worse, as she had suspected since her dawn waking on the marriage day of Colonel Fitzwilliam, the gaze was soon followed by the whisper of rumour and scandal. For why did Elizabeth sit alone? Where was Mr Darcy, cousin and boon companion of the groom, on such a day as this? Why did Mr Gresham have to stand in, as best man? – and so on.

Edward's absence, Elizabeth considered as she knelt, sat upright once more and pulled Miranda in closer, was easier to explain. His recent exposure as a ne'er-do-well – for thus she had heard her beloved son described by Miss Bingley, in low tones to Mrs Hurst – would travel no further than the family. However great the desire of Miss Bingley and her like to spread news of disaster and ruin, it was equally in their interests to remain silent: the slightest hint of disloyalty or rumour-mongering would be punished by Mr Darcy with the simplest and most easily administered of sentences, a lifelong exile from Pemberley. Lady Catherine, also, would enforce discretion. But none of this hindered the whispers – which swelled until Elizabeth could swear she had a sea of hostile speculation in the pews behind her, each monster that dwelt therein dreaming of a reason more grotesque for the absence of her husband than the last.

It did not improve matters that the two men who stood at the altar were both in love with the figure behind them, the solitary Elizabeth Darcy, who was responsible for all contingencies while Mr Darcy was away. Elizabeth prayed they would not look at her as they did; but Colonel Fitzwilliam, unaware at this moment, very probably, of the transparent emotions he betrayed, darted looks of such anguish and longing at her that she had recourse to lifting her prayer book in front of her face, that she might not be supposed to be returning them. Now, more than at any time since the early days of her marriage, Mrs Darcy must show the control of her feelings on which friends, servants and family had come to depend. That it was hard for her – for they had shared so much, she and the groom who would soon pledge to give all his support and affection to a stranger – she did not think anyone in the congregation was likely to suppose, for all the lively imagination that bred in the back pews of the chapel today. It had been assumed that Colonel Fitzwilliam's devotion was taken for granted by Mrs Darcy and her husband alike. But she knew – she knew only too well – of the times when Darcy's obstinacy over one matter or another had driven her to the company and attentions of his cousin; how near a close but unspoken relationship between them had come. She had seen her dear friend's eyes brim with tears on occasion – when Darcy had shown the icy manner that lay buried beneath the softened, loving exterior she had brought to being in him. She had wished as much as the faithful colonel to fling herself into his arms and sob her need for comfort. But she had desisted – as he respected her for doing, she knew – and, afraid of solitude and advancing years, he had chosen to marry in the end.

Lady Sophia, on the arm of a Major Farquhar, a distant cousin down from the north to give her away, now approached the aisle with a resolute step, and for a moment the eyes of the crowd turned to the bride. There was nothing to keep their gaze fixed on her, Elizabeth thought sadly: the betrothed of her closest friend, on the day that must be marked out as the most propitious in his life, had not taken the trouble to apply even a little powder, on this hot day – or even, as a whisper of surprise fled round the chapel at the apparition, bothered to dress her hair. This was unbrushed, with escaping strands caught in a garland of buttercups and daisies entwined; and it occurred to Elizabeth

106

that Lady Sophia might be taken for a woman escaped from an asylum, if it were not for the determination of her step, and her practical gaze. Her bridal smock, contrasted with the rich brocades and silks of those guests who found an invitation to Pemberley a rare honour, was little more than a night-shift. Yet – as Elizabeth considered, turning to smile at her new kinswoman, so that all the celebrants of the nuptial service should note her approval of Colonel Fitzwilliam's choice – why should Lady Sophia not be simple, if that was what she desired? There was less than two thousand a year, in the colonel's income from the farm; she brought nothing of her own; and her proclamation that she would make a fine farmer's wife should be greeted with relief rather than ridicule. Cheeks burning at her own superficial judgements of others, Elizabeth lowered her head; but not before, to her extreme embarrassment, she caught the eyes of the best man, Mr Gresham, at the altar fixed on her.

Elizabeth sang and prayed with the rest; and she could only register gratitude that her daughter, who was not of the type to pick up emotions easily, appeared to register nothing, despite her mother's flaming cheeks and tuneless voice, in the singing of the marriage hymns. Mr Gresham had no right to gaze at her in this way – if her cheeks burned now, it was because he appeared temporarily to have forfeited all sense of propriety. Unlike Colonel Fitzwilliam, who turned with a mild expression of anticipation, soon dashed, to his future wife as she came up the aisle, Mr Gresham announced, by the impertinence of his stare, by his flaunting of a handsome figure in a very fine blue coat, that showed his success and advancement as a leading architect and prospective Member of Parliament, his intention of becoming one day equal to the Darcys of Pemberley.

Mr Gresham took Elizabeth's blushes as a compliment, and as memento, also, doubtless, of their pleasant hour in the woods above Pemberley – for he pulled a white rose from his pocket, just as Colonel Fitzwilliam and his bride exchanged vows – and, by a sleight of hand that was all the more fetching for seeming to be utterly accidental, he spun the flower across the transept, to fall into Elizabeth's lap. A smile of such meaning followed this gesture, however, that the inhabitants of the pews behind the Darcy family row now turned their full attention away from the familiar rites at the altar, as practised by the parson with Colonel Fitzwilliam and Lady Sophia, and concentrated entirely upon the lovely and solitary figure of Mrs Darcy. New speculation as to the reason for her husband's absence began in a low tone and escalated to a tide of wonder. To make matters worse, Mr Gresham demonstrated his approval of this apprehension of a liaison between the wife of Mr Darcy and himself. He smiled, he came close to bowing to the inquisitive friends and family assembled there. A shaft of midsummer sun came in, and illuminated him, standing by the true couple; and there was not a single member of the wedding party able to deny he was a handsome fellow and deserved every happiness he could get.

So it is at weddings, as Elizabeth well knew; a collective lust for pleasure was ever near the surface, even if decorum kept it mostly buried; and the plighting of a dreary couple often led to a sense of excessive disappointment. But that *she* could stand in for the bride! – when her own mortification was so great she could only wish a hundred times she had not gone to walk in the woods, on an instinct she would for the rest of her days deplore. That her own marriage to Darcy appeared now to her and to everyone a matter of less interest than her possible new passions was too much to bear. She loved Darcy still; she could not have Gresham demonstrating his feelings like this, in public; and she prayed for the floor of the chapel to open up and take her down, for there she would at least find herself in a preferable Hell.

Mr Falk it was who leaned forward and alerted Elizabeth to a late arrival at the marriage ceremony in the chapel at Pemberley. No one knew why he had a seat in the second row; it was said by Miss Bingley to Mrs Hurst, but in confidence naturally, that the old man's attempts to educate Master Darcy having failed, he would not be a night longer at Pemberley; but tap her on the shoulder he did, while uttering the intelligence, in stentorian tones which paid no attention to the minute of silent prayer at this moment undertaken by the newly wedded couple, that Mrs Darcy was wanted in the vestibule, and without delay. A piece of crumpled paper in his hand bore out his news. Elizabeth rose, and, ignoring the ever brighter gaze of her guests, she crossed in front of the altar and made her way to the side door of the chapel and into the open air.

There was a long silence – then music rang out, for Colonel Fitzwilliam had engaged the brass of his old militia to make a fanfare of trumpets at the conclusion of the ceremony. That the side door should swing open, just as Colonel and Lady Sophia Fitzwilliam made their way up the aisle, towards the private entrance into Pemberley House, produced less surprise in the minds of those who had gathered together to bless the marriage than might at an earlier time in the proceedings have been the case – for there was no knowing, as Lady Catherine was heard to remark to her daughter in a tone of great disapproval, "what high jinks there may be now, at Pemberley".

In the event, the sight of a man and wife who had been married nineteen years could hardly be counted as scandalous. That they joined the happy couple and walked up the aisle behind Colonel Fitzwilliam and his wife with a quiet dignity commensurate with the manner to be expected of the oldest friends, cousins and patrons of the groom could only be considered right and proper. But that Mr Darcy and his wife smiled and pressed each other's hands like young lovers more eagerly back from the altar than the bride and groom seemed to the congregation to be remarkable indeed!

Twenty-two

More than once, in the glare and heat of the day that succeeded the marriage of Colonel Fitzwilliam, did Elizabeth attempt to draw Mr Darcy aside and discover the facts of his brief visit to London; but each time the happy couple – and this they were seen to be, far above the present groom and his new wife – made for a spot where they might be undisturbed, the restless crowd was either there before them, or directly after, with compliments, or enquiries as to the provenance of some of the fine objects now on display to mark the festive occasion. That Darcy avoided the close encounter did not occur to Elizabeth; and it was Jane, who was not capable of suspicion without the grounds for it, who came to express her concerns to her sister. Elizabeth stood in a group of admirers around a golden eagle, complete with jewelled wings, which had been placed at the end of the long gallery. Here Mr and Mrs Darcy greeted guests, who stood fixed in astonishment at the splendour of the great bird of prey before going on to ogle the fans, snuff-boxes and other treasures laid out in honour of Colonel Fitzwilliam and his bride.

"It is a gift from the Tsar of Russia," came the voice of Lady Catherine de Bourgh, who bore down on the group just as Jane reached Elizabeth's side. "The bird was considered vulgar in the extreme by my sister Lady Anne Darcy – but I dare say anything can be jumbled up alongside anything else these days. There is no style left; all is imitation and replica, and everywhere and everything is ransacked, whether Greece or Rome or Egypt, to provide the latest impression!"

"Lizzy!" said Jane in a low voice, as she saw her sister's eyes bright, looking up at Darcy as if he would give her all the information she needed, by the mere fact of begging for it with her gaze – "Lizzy, I pray you, take a walk with Darcy and insist on the truth!" Here Jane's voice grew lower still, as Miss Bingley approached, her features animated at the unexpected arrival of Mr Darcy at Pemberley – for, as she had many times informed those wedding guests who would stop for her, she had foreseen Mr Darcy in a carriage accident on the London road. That Pemberley would then be without a master she had not emphasised, for hints as to the unsuitability of Edward might result in this function proving to be the last to which she would receive an invitation.

"I own I thought myself at a country wedding today," said Miss Bingley in a very sweet voice, to Lady Catherine, but with her eyes fixed on Mr Darcy – and Elizabeth, not liking to spend time in the company of Miss Bingley, slipped to the side with her sister. "I could not tell the bride from a haystack, that was the difficulty!"

Mr Darcy, who did not wish to be deprived of the proximity of his wife, answered that Lady Sophia was a charming woman; and that he could not be more delighted for his cousin Fitzwilliam than he was today.

"My dear Darcy," said Lady Catherine, who now moved herself close to her nephew, obstructing Elizabeth completely from view, "I ask you, as your aunt, as the only representative of your dear mother's family, what you have learnt in London, of all the troubles that awaited you there."

Mr Darcy frowned at this; and Miss Bingley, who had also been pushed to the side by Lady Catherine, enquired of Mr Darcy if he would make a speech at the wedding, "or are the poor bridal couple to go without?"

Her plea went unheard, however – for Mrs Hurst, who came in search of her host and hostess, had many compliments to pay – as well as the desire, irrepressible in both of Charles Bingley's sisters, to administer a snub to persons considered inferior. In this case, the recipients of a patronising speech were Mr and Mrs Gardiner, Elizabeth's kindly aunt and uncle. The elderly couple, amazed by the new splendours on display at Pemberley, reiterated their joy at seeing such treasures revealed; and it was the sincere expression of these sentiments which gave Mrs Hurst her chance to humble the good pair in the presence of Mr Darcy. Remarking that "what you see is not a half of what is hidden here at Pemberley", and "it would surely have been in your power, dear Mr and Mrs Gardiner, to ask your beloved niece's husband at any time to open up the portfolios of drawings by Michelangelo and Leonardo in the library, for your even more private scrutiny", Mrs Hurst succeeded in causing distress to the Gardiners and in offending Mr Darcy. "I am pleased, nevertheless," continued Mrs Hurst, "to see the Raphael cartoons again, set up in the green drawing-room so excellently! I am sure it was Elizabeth who organised it all – and with the able assistance of Mr Gresham, I have little doubt!"

Mr Falk came up at this point; and it would have been hard to attribute the expression on Mr Darcy's face with certainty either to Mrs Hurst's remarks or to the presence of Mr Falk, whose impending dismissal from the Pemberley household was clear to all but himself.

"If Raphael had lived in England, he would have decorated Pemberley, just as in Rome he did the Vatican!" said Mrs Hurst, more loudly than she had intended, for her sayings were now succeeded by a profound silence. "Do not you agree, Caroline?"

Miss Bingley, who was seldom embarrassed, now shook her head in perplexity at her sister's perseverance – for Mr Darcy, who had smiled so happily on his return home, now stood glowering at the entire assembly – but she had nothing further to offer the company in the way of conversation other than that she had just heard of the creeping paralysis of another of Mrs Wilberforce's unfortunate daughters.

Mr Falk it was who put a stop both to Miss Bingley and to Mrs Hurst. "Raphael was employed to decorate the Vatican not because he was a great painter but because his uncle was architect to the Pope," announced the old tutor, and, downing a glass of punch which was demonstrably not his first, he walked with an unsteady gait down the long gallery.

113

After this, the group dispersed and Mr Darcy went in search of his wife.

Elizabeth and Jane had by now retired to a small cabinet that led from the long gallery, and had thus missed the humiliation of the Gardiners as well as Mr Falk's impudent interjection. Yet, as if he had divined their need to be alone together, the sisters found themselves waylaid by Thomas Roper: he wished to lecture them on all the precious possessions now brought from the vaults, to mark the marriage of Colonel Fitzwilliam; and, despite Mrs Darcy's assurances that she knew the contents of her own home as well as anyone, he had only given way when Miranda appeared in the crowd, and was deemed a suitable recipient for his lecture. It was with a pang that Elizabeth had allowed him to take Miranda off in search of a knowledge she had had by heart, since childhood, rather than invite her daughter to accompany them to a quiet place away from the wedding guests. But Jane spoke with an urgency which was rare for her; it would not be right for Miranda to hear her parents' marriage discussed – for this, Elizabeth knew as well as she knew her own sister, was the reason for Jane's sudden decision to speak with her.

Today, Elizabeth reflected, Jane was more lovely than ever; and thinking of their father – for the library at Pemberley had been remodelled in memory of Mr Bennet, and they stood in a small room adjacent to that splendid chamber, domed and pillared as befitted the magnificent collection housed within – Elizabeth decided that he would have been proud to know her, as she was in her maturity. Jane was in white, with green ornaments; her style of dress had changed, as had to be, with the passing of the years – but green was as ever her favourite colour, and she became it as never before. Her goodness, and her patience in dealing with all the obstacles life had set in front of her, had given a dignity to her beauty. Her head was set very high on her shoulders; her eyes, soft and clear, looked reproach at Elizabeth.

The sisters went to the window, which gave on to the lawns and gardens of Pemberley. If a visitor, an artist perhaps, or merely an onlooker with an eye for beauty – someone, in short, a long way in temperament from a preponderance of the acquaintance gathered today for the wedding party – had seen them there, then Elizabeth would most probably appear the superior of the two; for, although she did not possess the regularity of features which so distinguished Jane from other women, her intelligence gave an added dimension to her charms. Her yellow silk dress – which she wore for Darcy, even though imagining he would be absent, for she knew he loved her in yellow and had caused her to be painted in this bright Chinese hue, her children playing at her side, on the Palladian bridge at Pemberley – gave colour to her bright eyes and face. She was taller than Jane, by a little, and her figure, unchanged by childbearing, was as slight as the day Darcy had refused her as a dancing companion, many years ago, at Netherfield. Recalling that – for Elizabeth was sad to think of her father, and all he missed in his two eldest daughters – brought a slight smile to her lips, though she tried to look as serious as she could, to hear Jane's remonstrances.

"Lizzy, you *must* discover from Darcy what has become of Edward!" Jane's voice was strained, and it was clearly difficult for her to proceed. "And the gambling debts! You must *insist* that he take you aside – surely, Lizzy, just for a few minutes, whether he acts the host or not! Edward is your son! Are you not frantic with worry, Eliza dearest?"

Elizabeth felt herself grow pale – but Jane could not be refused an honest answer. Gently, hoping for more understanding than she could ever obtain, even from her loved sister, she told of the years of anguish she had suffered since Edward had first shown his disaffection, when he was all of seven years old; that she was accustomed to harden her heart against news of him, in case it was bad – "and anyway, Jane, Darcy told me I have nothing to fear. Edward is safe. Those were his words. Is it not kinder to poor Colonel Fitzwilliam to permit him his day of happiness . . .?"

"If such it is," said Jane, with a glance at Elizabeth. "At least you say Edward is safe, though."

"Thank God," said Elizabeth in a low voice that was none the less heartfelt for its muted pitch. "Please, Jane, believe me! Darcy will tell me when he chooses to – when the time is right!"

"Elizabeth, you are become far too acquiescent, as Darcy's wife. Where is the spirit you once possessed? All the impatience, to discover what was hidden from you? I recall occasions – "

But here Lady Sophia Fitzwilliam, evidently also seeking sanctuary from the throng, and equally evidently dismayed to find herself not alone, came into the cabinet, and there was the need for compliments to be presented on the ceremony, and wishes for future joy, and all this was then succeeded by talk of the weather, and the possibility of thunder, and the price of rams.

The opportunity was gone, Elizabeth saw, for Jane to upbraid her further – and partially she was glad, for her sister had gone too near the truth for it to be comfortable. It was certain, by now – Jane was more modern, more free, in her marriage, than she. But then, with a secret delight which could not be divulged even to the sister and friend closest to her in the world, Elizabeth placed the responsibility for *that* with Mr Darcy.

Twenty-three

Till Elizabeth entered the long gallery once more, and took her place at Darcy's side, she had not admitted to herself that Jane was right, and she must glean all the information she needed from him, without delay.

All her mind was now taken up with memories of Edward, and painful suspicions that she would never be with him again. The absence of the boy – which had duly been noted by the wedding guests, as Elizabeth, attuned over many years to the pitch and whine of gossip and malice, was uncomfortably aware – now became to her a lack so obvious, and so intolerable, that she wondered at her own defence of Darcy, to her sister. She *must* know where he was; and the clear anticipation of those who, like Miss Bingley and Mrs Hurst, awaited final confirmation of the pollution of the shades of Pemberley, as prophesied by Lady Catherine at the time of Elizabeth and Darcy's marriage, made matters worse still. If he was in prison, seized for debt – she must know it. If he was safe, as Mr Darcy assured her, where was he hiding? Snatches of the boy's letters home brought fresh anguish to Elizabeth, as they floated across her mind: new phrases he used with pride; he was "full of beans", he said, and sent regards to his favourite horse. Elizabeth had much to do to control her tears; for the last thing she desired, while she knew she was considered to blame for the criminal acts – by reason of birth, ill management, over-indulgence and all the other sins – of her poor son, was to be found weeping like a weak, lost mother. She would not give them the pleasure of seeing her thus; and a part of her, also, believed that it must all be a mistake; that Edward had been taken for another; and

117

that he was still at school, working to gain the fine education for which his parents yearned. That the lad must have lied to them, on the subject of his scholarship, was too painful to consider; that the losing of ten thousand acres in Wales was his mark of distinction now was too incredible to swallow without further enquiry of Darcy – who stood smiling beside her as he greeted and spoke to the guests.

Elizabeth took the decision to go outside, to satisfy her urgent need for news of Edward – but this entailed going out on the parterre at the head of a long train of guests, all of whom were eager to follow Mrs Darcy and her husband to any delightful spot in the Pemberley grounds. However fast Elizabeth walked – and she had Darcy's arm, she would not let him go – she could not shake off her role as hostess and guide. The cascade was particularly admired; and they had all to stand some minutes, as Thomas Roper, who had joined the party without delay, explained the methods of his new calculating machine and the measurements of the water, as it fell from step to step on the great stone staircase. They went to the park, where Darcy and his new bride had, eighteen years ago, planted trees from tropical climes – from China, the spiked witch hazel, from Japan the flowering prunus which had only its equal at Kew – and here, too, Mr Roper delivered his lectures on the upkeep and maintenance of an arboretum. If Elizabeth had not suffered such impatience to hear the worst – for she believed now that Mr Darcy concealed a tragedy from her, both to save her from pain and to avoid the spoiling of Colonel Fitzwilliam's marriage day – she would have smiled at the absurdity of it all. But she noted, with some pride at the evident sensibility of her daughter, that Miranda did not smile, either; that she looked towards her mother with sympathy and affection; and that Mr Roper's attentions, one hundred times more annoying for her than was the mere observation of him, for Elizabeth, were not at this instance to be taken as a subject for laughter between mother and daughter. Roper could not, of course, know of the disgrace of Edward; but his proprietorial attitude to the trees, artefacts and very grass of the park at Pemberley, while

118

patently affording amusement to Mr Darcy, only served to underline the horror of the situation. She *would* find somewhere to speak with her husband – Jane had guessed rightly that it was he who evaded his own wife, though seemingly so close to her, in public – and in desperation she turned back towards the house, the ever-growing throng following her with the obedience of a flock of well-trained sheep.

Now the canopies outside the west wing came into sight, and under them tables, decorated with garlands of flowers and leaves, covered over with tablecloths of finest lawn. Tea and cakes and ices were in the process of being demolished, mostly by the ancient and the very young among the guests – and for a moment Elizabeth forgot her troubles, to survey a scene that was a perfect picture of a summer wedding. The day was fine and warm, the sky blue, and the only interruption of happiness a swarm of small bees – which were soon chased away, to settle on the lilies and roses Elizabeth had propagated and tended at Pemberley since coming here as wife of Mr Darcy. It was a temptation to linger here, and to refuse the intelligence which must be learnt and understood.

A murmur of approval went up at the appearance of Colonel Fitzwilliam and his bride, who came into the tea garden with expressions of pure pleasure at the efforts made for their sake alone. Better still, Elizabeth noted a look of real affection pass between the colonel and Lady Sophia – and here, as she castigated herself for all her frivolity and love of hiding away from truth, Elizabeth could scourge herself further for her deliberate lack of sympathy for her old friend and his choice of a wife. They loved each other – they had very likely as firm an understanding as Elizabeth had found with her own husband. Of all those who would come forward with practical assistance and support once the news of Edward was out, it would not surprise her to find Lady Sophia in the forefront of loyal friends. Elizabeth was too prone to judge, and to judge too impulsively – she would be humbled, when the truth was out, and she would not permit herself such prejudice again.

Mr Darcy smiled still at everyone who came near him – whether to make up for the scowls brought about by Miss Bingley and Mrs Hurst, or simply as a way of hiding his own very great distress, it was impossible to tell – but he did, in any event, allow himself to be led by Elizabeth away from the innocent pleasures of the garden to a high part of the grounds behind the house. They were soon on a bridge, which passed under a tunnel, thence turning to a muddy path mostly trodden by the gardeners and servants of Pemberley. Elizabeth went there, often, to the kitchen garden; she loved the neat rows of vegetables, the air of tranquillity and peace; but she sensed her husband had not visited the place since he was a child; and, for all her concern over their son, she could not help herself smiling up at him. If only they had come here together, in the past – for she could see he was enchanted by the place, with its high brick walls and newly dug beds, glistening brown earth, with evidence of meticulous care to both root and leaf; but Darcy had always too much to attend to – he was too preoccupied with the management of so many lives and so much land – and it was this, perhaps, also, which had caused the change in Edward, his strangeness, his pretence of his mother's family as foreigners, his dislike of his own name – for she had given the major portion of her thoughts and attention to his father, and not to him.

"You seem unlike yourself, dearest, loveliest Elizabeth," said Darcy, in a voice so tender that Elizabeth recalled with pain that it was a long time since she had heard him address her thus. "You imagine I have something to tell you which will bring you great unhappiness. But it is not so. The scamps are apprehended; Edward was led astray by young Althorp; they fell into the hands of moneylenders, but a word with his father sufficed – the Brecon estates are safe!"

Elizabeth did not dare look at her husband again, and her eyes fell on the gravel path, with its neat border of box hedge. Some pebbles had been disturbed by Darcy's tread, and with the point of her shoe she realigned them.

"And Edward?" she said in so low a voice she could imagine it inaudible to him.

"He lodges with his housemaster, at school; he has given his word that he will continue with his studies, and that he will have no more to do with these rascals," said Darcy, and this time he bent to kiss Elizabeth, and to cup her chin in his hands, so that her gaze must come up to meet his. "He is repentant; you will see him when he comes here in the holidays. He is ashamed, and he loves you – he will write to you, my lovely Eliza, and he bids you, as I do, not to fret over him any more."

"So they take him back, without considering expulsion?" cried Elizabeth, and at last she wept, with the relief of it all.

"They would not consider expelling him," said Darcy; and now with his added assurances that all was well and as it had been before the wedding party had got under way at Pemberley, and with talk of the plans he had made for their journey to Venice and their sojourn there, Elizabeth could begin to believe that it had all been a bad dream, in actuality; and that she could not wait to tell Jane, and to weep a little on her shoulder as well, now all her worst fears were proved unfounded.

"My aunt Catherine will be happy to hear that we have our estates in Wales, still," said Darcy; and Elizabeth heard the laughter and gaiety in his voice, now all the peccadilloes of his son had been corrected, and no grievous harm done. "Though she did not once, in all the time my mother was alive, find the time to leave Rosings and visit us there!"

Elizabeth smiled at this. Slowly, and closely entwined, she and Darcy left the enclave of the kitchen garden, to rejoin the wedding party, for there was the dinner banquet to come, which they must preside over; and then fireworks and music, before the celebrations of the day were done. The day was fading a little, into an evening of scented roses and the first hint of dusk – and it was only as she and Darcy emerged from the low tunnel on to the wooden bridge over the stream which fed the vegetable garden that she thought to ask him further of the nature of the rogues who had corrupted their son.

"A terrible old woman, if you care to believe it!" replied

Darcy, with a laugh. "A woman who has fallen into disrepute; she encourages the scions of great houses to gamble and drink; and she is no longer received anywhere. Lady Harcourt is her name!"

Part Three

Twenty-four

Mrs Bennet's return to Hertfordshire was marked by an unusual absence of information as to the extent of the pleasure of her visit to London; and whether Harcourt House had lived up to her expectations was not known for several days after Meryton Lodge was reliably reported to be occupied once more by Mrs Bennet and her youngest daughter. Unable to contain her curiosity, or to await an invitation to see her old friend, Mrs Long set off early one day, in the hope of receiving confidences which might otherwise go to Lady Lucas or Mrs Collins – though both these ladies professed themselves also mystified by Mrs Bennet's lack of a social call, at just the time when they had been awaiting one. No one liked to say that Mrs Bennet was more welcome now, to visit them, than she had been before her departure for London, for now she had something to impart, other than speculation on the nature of her new relation; and no one was prepared to join this unuttered remark with the further observation that the trip to London must have resulted in disappointment, rather than success.

Mrs Bennet, when brought downstairs at the butler's announcing of Mrs Long, was quick to dispel any such notion, even before the possibility of its being suggested.

"I did not call on you, my dear Mrs Long, for fear of tiring you with excessive detail – of the magnificence of my hostess's appointments and furnishings, which I feared also might bring a sense of inferiority to those of us who live simply at Meryton and do not have access to the splendours of Harcourt House!"

Mrs Long replied that she considered herself capable of

surviving Mrs Bennet's descriptions; and wondered if Mrs Bennet now felt herself in an infinitely lower order of things, since her return from London.

"Certainly I do not, Mrs Long! My house may be small, but it is appointed by the upholsterers and curtain-makers to Mrs Darcy of Pemberley! Nothing is too good for Meryton Lodge; and I am surprised you have not seen that, I may say. Indeed, when I am asked to supply a description of my home to a stranger, I give the Maison de Pompadour as an example – in the woods at Fontainebleau, a charming small lodge, and the gift of King Louis to Madame de Pompadour herself!"

"Was Lady Harcourt informed of this likeness?" enquired Mrs Long, for she now fancied that Mrs Bennet's head had been turned by her sojourn in London, and that she might be in need of medical attention.

Mrs Long's insistence on receiving particulars of Lady Harcourt, whether in cunningly posed questions such as the one just formed, or in out-and-out questioning, went unsatisfied; and Mrs Bennet was now asked once more to enumerate the glories of the house, and its actual position. Mrs Long, who was not considered a fool in the town, began to grow suspicious. "Why, there were as many paintings by Sir Joshua Reynolds as you can imagine, going all the way up the stairs," cried Mrs Bennet. "The curtains are of damask and as high as a waterfall – Oh, Lydia" – for here Lydia came into the room, and Mrs Long caught an appealing look in Mrs Bennet's eye as she greeted her daughter – "I was telling Mrs Long of all the splendours of Harcourt House – yet I cannot do justice to them, indeed I cannot! Was the great picture on the stairs by Van Dyck or by Thomas Gainsborough? Was it of the late Sir William Harcourt? My retention of detail becomes excessively poor, the older I grow, my dear Mrs Long; yet we must all suffer these lapses as best we can, for we enter old age equipped with little but our fond memories – and then these are taken from us, as well!"

Mrs Long was unimpressed by this summing-up of the indignities of age, and moved with alacrity to the subject of the wedding to which Mrs Bennet and Mrs Wickham had been invited.

"Why, we nearly didn't get there at all!" said Mrs Bennet. "Our carriage was caught in such a crush, and I do believe we were swept down a street called Berwick, before we could extricate ourselves."

"But is not St James's Church in Piccadilly prominent in the extreme?" enquired Mrs Long. "I may not jaunt about as you do, my dear Mrs Bennet, but, as you know, I have a niece who writes to me from the Regent's Park – and she has laid it all out quite clearly, for me best to understand her social engagements, and where they lead her. St James's is opposite Albany, a very fine building, I am informed!"

"My mother makes a mistake," Lydia cut in, for she had observed Mrs Long's desire to seek further for the truth of the visit. "The wedding was indeed in a church, as previously arranged. A cousin of Lady Harcourt's, a young man – "

"Of what profession?" pounced Mrs Long.

"I believe . . ." began Lydia, but she faltered as she spoke, "yes, I believe he was in the militia, Mrs Long!"

"Then he wore the insignia," said Mrs Long, for it was clear to her by now that something was concealed from her. "Was it the dragoons, Mrs Wickham? I believe you would know *that*, if nothing else – for everyone in the locality was aware of you and your sister Kitty's predilection for dragoons, all those many years ago!"

Lydia faltered once more, and said she did not recall well enough to which regiment the groom belonged.

"For it was dark," cried Mrs Bennet, as if her faculties had just that moment been restored to her. "It was too dark to see, Mrs Long – why, we could not see the bride clearly – could we, Lyddy? It was most annoying, when Lady Harcourt had assured us in her letters that her cousin married a young woman of great beauty and impeccable breeding!"

Mrs Long rose, saying she had errands to complete in the town. As the weather continued warm, it was best to buy fish just a matter of hours before consumption, and she had no wish to poison Major and Miss Merriman, this evening, for all that Miss Merriman had robbed her at whist last week at Lady Lucas's.

"I may call on Lady Lucas, also," said Mrs Long, as she took her leave. "She will be most intrigued to hear how *dark* London has become, at three in the afternoon and in the height of summer! She may prevent Sir William from returning there – if the climate is become as insalubrious as you say!"

"Whatever do you mean, Mrs Long?" said poor Mrs Bennet, who now wished only to know where she had blundered.

But Mrs Long reiterated her desire to pay a call on Lady Lucas, even if she carried wet fish in her bag and did not go a roundabout way to take it home first. "This is a very serious matter, Mrs Bennet. I believe dear Charlotte should be apprised also, so that she may decide whether or not to trouble Mrs Darcy and Mrs Bingley at this time of the glorious celebration of the marriage of Colonel Fitzwilliam. It is my duty to inform Mrs Collins – then it is of course entirely her decision as to the course she and Mr Collins will pursue."

Mrs Long went down the drive with more than her customary speed, and turned in the direction of the Lucases' house – for she had already determined to put off the fish until later, however unfortunate the consequences.

Mrs Bennet, meanwhile, when she gave up demanding where she had betrayed the true nature of their visit, sat on in silence; and all Lydia's counting of the trophies she had brought back with her from London, and the laying out of boxes and fans on the sitting-room floor, could not raise her mother from her gloom.

Twenty-five

Jane and Elizabeth went on the following day to the moors above Matlock; the gig which had brought them from Pemberley waited at the foot of the expanse of grass, bracken and ling that made up this wild spot; and both expressed a delight at the change of scenery and air the excursion provided. Jane was to return to Yorkshire with her family on the next day, and she would take Miss Bingley with her – for all that, the house had still Lady Catherine as a guest, and Miss de Bourgh, whose efforts on the piano the evening before had been a trial to all those of the wedding guests who remained. Mr Roper had also requested that he stay on, supported in this by Lady Catherine; and Darcy, whose geniality was generally remarked on, had granted him an extension of his time at Pemberley.

Compared to such a medley – and with the house constantly receiving visitors to the lower gallery, where Colonel Fitzwilliam's wedding gifts were on display – the loneliness and emptiness of the moors were delicious to Elizabeth. Like Jane, she had little time that could be seen as her own, for she had promised to call on the colonel and his bride, in their farmhouse below, and to spend a short while with them, leaving Jane to return to Pemberley in the gig. But each minute that she breathed in the moorland air she felt freedom from the constraints and fears of the past days: here, indeed, the misdemeanours of Edward took on their rightful proportion, and her own and Darcy's happiness and good fortune could be seen, like the vast horizon that lay before her, as limitless. Jane had been right, as so often before: Elizabeth was too impulsive, too quick to believe the worst; and, even if it were true that a period in the past that had contained little but worry about the child and fear for his future had formed a habit in her of expecting the worst that could befall, she was only like other mothers in this. Jane was an exception, she knew – for her calm would not be ruffled, however imminent disaster in the rearing of children might appear.

"I speculate sometimes that I was not born for the maternal role," said Elizabeth, laughing. She and her sister now stood at the highest point of the moor, and could look across the great expanse of land that separated them from the wooded hills above Pemberley. The Hunting Tower, small as a house for children, was visible in the far woods; but Elizabeth put her mind away from Mr Gresham, and her walk on that day of midsummer – so short a time in the past, and yet so distant, for by now the wedding was completed, Darcy was back in place at Pemberley, and no harm had come to his estates or his son.

"Indeed you are mistaken, Lizzy!" replied Jane, in the warmest tones. "Your son loves you – Edward was heartbroken when it was considered time for him to go south to school!"

Elizabeth sighed at these words, and vowed to herself that she would spend more time with Edward in the holidays – for without Colonel Fitzwilliam the boy would be sadly unoccupied. The colonel and Lady Sophia – who had reiterated her husband's sincere invitation that the boy come for as many weeks as he liked, to walk up the birds and fish the river at Matlock – must not have him too long. Yet, as Elizabeth considered Edward and the contentment he evinced when encouraged in country pursuits, she knew she would see little of him, and she mourned the fact. The boy did not need his mother – he needed his father to join with him as sportsman and friend. Elizabeth prayed that this latest fright, with Darcy's only son, would persuade him of this, and that he would open up to the lad. Perhaps when Edward is older, thought Elizabeth, who then found herself thinking that this had been her prayer for as many years as she could recall.

"As for Miranda, she is such a clever mingling of her

mother and father that I never can decide which she takes after the most!" said Jane. "I think Darcy, probably – and she has her father's loyal admiration for you, Lizzy!"

"You are flattering me over much, dearest Jane," said Elizabeth – who took her sister's hand suddenly, as she had been wont to do as a child, and leapt down through the grass and heather, in a final gesture of her desire for freedom, and her need to live and breathe, on just this one fine, faultless day, under a blue northern sky without thoughts of husband, son or daughter.

"If there is someone with little knowledge of the maternal role, then I fear it is poor Mama," said Jane, when both sisters stood within sight of the gig – which had grown proportionally bigger as they descended, and thus served as a reminder of the duties ahead and of the reality of the day.

"Poor Mama," said Elizabeth; and as they crossed a small beck that ran through the rough terrain she pulled Jane down, again with a childish lack of restraint, that they might dabble their fingers in the clear water running over brown stones. "I have written to Charlotte – to our old friend Charlotte Lucas, Jane, who is as ever the patient wife of Mr Collins . . ."

Here Jane and her sister joined in laughing again, and only returned to gravity when the figure of Colonel Fitzwilliam, stiff and dependable as he would always be, whether lately wed or not, appeared on the track beneath them. He feared for the safety of Elizabeth too much – she was aware of that – and today he seemed to her simply another fetter in her life of loves and responsibilities – a life she had so violently wished not to lose, when it was threatened by forces beyond her control, but from which, now it was restored to her in full, she savoured the rare escape.

"I have asked Charlotte to discover how Mama came to make the acquaintance of this Lady Harcourt – for you told me of her, Jane, some days back, but the preparations for the wedding, and all the rest, quite put it out of my mind."

Elizabeth went on to explain to her sister all the information – which, as she recounted it, she saw was pitifully sparse – that Darcy had given her in the kitchen garden at Pemberley on the day of the wedding feast. Jane frowned as she heard the tale; and, when it was done, her first comment was on her sister's ability to take charge of such a matter by writing to Charlotte – when she, Jane, would as likely as not have no notion at all of how to go about discovering any more on the friendship of Lady Harcourt and their poor deluded mother.

"Indeed, you would, Jane!" said Elizabeth sharply. "I fear Mama may be in danger. This woman Harcourt is most disreputable, and goes for Edward and the Darcy fortune – why would she wish to make the acquaintance of our mother, unless it were in some way connected with all this?"

"Have you told Darcy of your suspicions?" said Jane. "Now I fear for Mama also!"

Elizabeth replied, but without looking at Jane, that she had not informed Darcy of Mrs Bennet's new association. There was no need for an explanation of this lack, between them – though Jane said she thought it necessary, if they were to save their mother from harm.

"I cannot, Jane," said Elizabeth in a low voice, as Colonel Fitzwilliam came up over the steep ground towards them, dislodging a small avalanche of stones as he walked.

"But you *must*, Lizzy!" Jane said in a whisper, as the colonel arrived to stand over them, with the triumphant air of a dog which has found a lost walker in the snow. "Promise me you will!"

For all the colonel's jocose enquiries as to the nature of the promise that was the subject of Jane's pleas, both sisters were silent on the walk down to the waiting gig. Colonel Fitzwilliam offered a visit to the farmhouse to Mrs Bingley – "for my wife has all her rugs down now, y'know, and her pictures on the walls" – and without noticing the heightened colour of Mrs Bingley and Mrs Darcy, and their efforts not to burst out laughing, the good colonel proceeded to enumerate several other innovations at the farmhouse at Matlock.

Jane replied to his invitation by insisting quietly that she must return to Pemberley, to prepare for her journey to Yorkshire the following day; and after waving her sister farewell, as she set off in the gig, Elizabeth accompanied the colonel to his matrimonial home.

Twenty-six

Elizabeth had no sooner entered the farmhouse above Matlock than she came to feel – more strongly than before – that she had judged Lady Sophia on first acquaintance in a manner that was definitely superficial and hasty.

The farmhouse, now that it showed the occupancy of a wife to Colonel Fitzwilliam, could not be described as well furnished – or even comfortable, for the curtains, unlined and of the most inexpensive cotton, hung with an almost forlorn air by the side of the windows, while the rag rugs on the flagstone floor gave credibility to the reason for their previous owners' being prepared to part with them, without financial reward. Each chair contained a dog, whose deposits, Elizabeth had been startled to note, remained in the front hall and had not been cleaned up – and only the intense cold alleviated the odour which was the natural result of this oversight – and each dog leapt down to greet the mistress of Pemberley, none of them called off, even by Colonel Fitzwilliam, who looked to his wife to perform this function, but in vain.

Lady Sophia did not invite Elizabeth to sit down; and, once she had stroked and greeted the dogs, and a modicum of calm had been returned to the room, there was little to do but wonder at the Spartan existence that must have been the lot of the colonel's wife as a child – for all the splendours of Castle Farquhar, as denoted by Miss Caroline Bingley at the time of the wedding. Lady Sophia was more like a savage than a child was – this Elizabeth could not help but reflect – she had not been reared at all, and that must be the truth of it.

Reflections on rearing children were not, however, agreeable to Elizabeth, and she tried, though with little success, to imagine that Lady Sophia's awkward exterior hid a heart of gold. That this was not the case was borne out an instant later, when Elizabeth, shown to a chair by a beaming Colonel Fitzwilliam, found the superficiality of her judgement of the wife of Darcy's cousin lay in an excess of charity, rather than the other way about. It was once again incomprehensible to Elizabeth that so good-natured and delightful a man as Colonel Fitzwilliam should have bound himself to one such as Lady Sophia – and be perfectly happy with his decision, by all appearances.

Elizabeth, who saw that her old friend was oblivious to the lack of hospitality on Lady Sophia's part – for there was no offer of tea, or of refreshment of any kind – determined to stay as short a time as possible at Matlock. She wished earnestly that she had accompanied Jane to Pemberley: *there* was comfort and warmth and brightness, all from the natural splendour of the place and the loving heart of Mr Darcy and Miranda; *here* was scorn, if the lack of civility on Lady Sophia's part could so be described. The chill in the house, which seemed to have retained winter temperatures within the stone walls, despite the glorious summer's day outside, emphasised the disagreeable sense of being in the company of a cold-blooded creature, rather than a human being; and Elizabeth promised herself she would depart just as soon as her feelings of duty and loyalty to Colonel Fitzwilliam would permit.

"The storm we have been expecting will come tonight," said Colonel Fitzwilliam – for it seemed to Elizabeth he did not wish to broach the subject of Edward's gambling in London and the outcome of Mr Darcy's visit, however eager he might be to learn the facts. "There will be thunder, and the cattle will need to be brought down into the shed. I expect Miss Darcy will see to the herd at Pemberley, for old Mr Gresham still lies at death's door, I believe."

"It is to be hoped there will not be too costly a funeral for an estate manager, such as Mr Gresham," said Lady Sophia.

"You may be aware, Mrs Darcy, that in Scotland there is no church service or any other folderol, when a man dies, however distinguished his station. Mourners gather by the open grave, a prayer is said – that is all!"

Elizabeth said she had not yet given consideration to the obsequies of old Mr Gresham – but as the very mention of the name brought shameful colour to her cheeks, she added hastily that she was happy to impart the news that Edward would be at Pemberley in the holidays – and she was certain he would wish to accept the colonel's and Lady Sophia's kind offer to fish and shoot with them. If Elizabeth did speculate as to where the boy would find a morsel to eat, in so parsimonious a household, she did not, naturally, say anything on the subject; but, as Lady Sophia's further remarks were at first not believable to her, she did think, for what seemed an eternity, that her cousin's new wife had divined her dislike for her, and was as outspoken on the subject of the boy as guest at Matlock as she might not unreasonably be.

"I do not expect Edward Darcy here, Mrs Darcy! I do not believe he will come here, this summer – or go to Yorkshire, for the grouse shoot, either!"

Colonel Fitzwilliam looked so miserable at his wife's pronouncements that Elizabeth came to realise, with a jolt of horror, that her old friend knew something she did not – that Darcy had confided in him, in a way he would never find possible with *her* – and, to make matters worse, both Colonel Fitzwilliam and Lady Sophia were under the impression she *had* been told, and had invited her to Matlock in all probability to talk over the matter. The absence of refreshments, the colonel's over-affable manner, all spelt some kind of disaster to Elizabeth now.

"Why – what has happened?" was all she could in the end produce – and she saw, in a moment she would never erase from her mind – the brief look of satisfaction in the eyes of Lady Sophia, as she composed her reply.

"Edward has been disinherited by his father, Mrs Darcy! We thought you must be aware of it! Mr Darcy's visit to London was for that purpose."

"And to save the estates in Wales," said Colonel Fitzwilliam. "All are safe now, dear cousin Elizabeth"; and the good man, with evident sincerity, came forward to comfort her.

"But . . ." said Elizabeth, for she trembled despite herself, and felt the presence of Lady Sophia as a reason to control herself, for she would rather die than break down while observed by her. "Where is Edward? Darcy said he was safe . . ."

"I do not believe Darcy saw his son," said Colonel Fitzwilliam quietly; "he was aware of the priority – "

"– of saving the estates," cried Elizabeth with bitterness.

"By settling the matter with the father of young Althorp, Mr Darcy also prevented the seizure of Master Darcy for debt," said Colonel Fitzwilliam, and now a tone of mild reproach could be detected in his delivery. "Edward is indeed safe – from prison, dear cousin Elizabeth. Will that not do?"

Twenty-seven

The first drops of rain came down as Elizabeth reached the gates of Pemberley; and, as she thanked the farm boy who had brought her in the pony and cart from Matlock, her first thought was that the lad would return home drenched to the skin. He was slight in build, and had a tousled head, like Edward: perhaps, she thought as she clambered from the trap, she felt for him in this way because she had just learnt of the final disgrace of her son; whatever the reason, she extracted a promise from him not to go under trees on the way home, if the thunder that rolled still far off in the sky grew nearer – and to wait until the storm had passed, before he presented himself at Colonel Fitzwilliam's door.

That there was a worse storm brewing, in her heart, Elizabeth had no doubt. She had long known her son's defects, it was true – and she had long suspected, also, that Edward would fall prey to the weaker side of his nature many times over, before arriving at maturity – she had prepared herself for all this, and a hundred times imagined the pleas that would be made to Darcy to give his son another chance. To permit him the life for which he had been readied, as soon as he was born – was this too much to ask? But to banish him – just like that, as Elizabeth perceived it – to remove him, as she had always feared her husband would, from the family altogether, and leave him a waif, homeless, almost without a name – this she had not foreseen.

The thought was horrible to contemplate, and Elizabeth, who had insisted on disembarking from the Fitzwilliams' rough conveyance by the gates, now walked down through the park and found herself glad of the increasing darkness, the thunderous night overtaking summer's evening, which the storm, as it came over the wooded hills behind her, seemed anxious to provide. How could she look on the gardens – the placid lake, where her uncle Gardiner would sit, if the day had not grown so intemperate, the roses and topiary and walks of hazel and willow – when she knew her own son banned from them for ever? And how could she forgive Darcy – this she could not even entertain, that it would ever be possible – not only for the act of disinheriting his own flesh and blood, but for putting such an act in train without consulting her at all! And that he should return for his cousin's wedding, and smile at all the guests – and woo her too! – she suffered at the thought of it – with promises of their fine journey to Italy! Indeed, he was in good humour – he had safeguarded his estates, he had rid himself of the burden of Edward, and Edward's proclivities, for the rest of his days! But he need not imagine his wife would love him for that – there, Elizabeth thought, her face grim as she ran the last steps, with rain now falling fast on parterre and steps, over the bridge and towards the west door of the house – there he was mistaken, and she would inform him of *that* without delay!

The footman, admitting Elizabeth, when attempting to take her rain-soaked cloak, was asked of Mr Darcy's whereabouts in a tone unknown to him from the sweet-natured lady of the house; and in his consternation he replied, stumbling over his words, that Mr Darcy was in the library, and in an hour he departed for Kympton – or so it was said.

Elizabeth reining herself in, as she had trained herself to do, saw she had alarmed the man, and now thanked him with her accustomed kindness.

Mr Darcy stood in the library with his back to the fireplace – as if, Elizabeth thought in her sorrow and shame, he staked out the ownership of Pemberley in perpetuity. Edward would never stand here. After Darcy there was no line in sight; and the fact of her husband's being in his coat and holding his riding-crop gave an air of siege to his appearance there. He would fend off any person who questioned his stance – so he seemed to announce; he dressed both for the defending of his land and for the protection of his home.

Elizabeth did not pause, seeing him there; though she did wonder, when he did not greet her, whether many another would run the gauntlet of Mr Darcy's anger.

"I am come from Matlock," said Elizabeth; "and I hear of your actions. You will justify them, if you can – "

"I have no need to justify my actions," Darcy replied in a tone so cold that Elizabeth saw the futility of approaching him; and her heart sank accordingly.

"You may recall, my dear Elizabeth, the strictures of my aunt Catherine at the time of our son's first foolish outbursts – "

"I do *not* care to recall the words of a woman who knows nothing of gentleness, or softness," said Elizabeth; and her own anger now made her every minute less soft, in tone and colour.

"I was warned of the failing within your family, before we were wed, Elizabeth. My deepest regret is that I proceeded with my proposal of marriage, to you."

"My failing?" cried Elizabeth.

"Mrs Bennet makes as fine a proof of madness as any I have yet met," said Darcy. "Lady Catherine spoke of it; and there is an imbalance in her relations, wherever they are encountered."

"An imbalance indeed!" cried Elizabeth. "It has been *your* responsibility that Edward is of an unbalanced disposition. You could not give him affection. You care only for inheritance and money – "

"And that, alas, is where Edward is involved," said Darcy, with a smile so hateful that Elizabeth ran towards him, her hand raised.

There was no need to wait, before administering a slap to the cheek of Mr Darcy – for, sidestepping her with a further smirk of superiority, he left the library, and she heard him call for John, and the great door in the hall slam behind him.

That he had received further and even more unpalatable news of his son than the gaming and debauch already dealt with in London must surely be the case; but Elizabeth's mind was in turmoil – she hated him, at last, and she could think only of his sweet words in the kitchen garden and his casual dismissal of the misdeeds of his son.

Miranda will know, thought Elizabeth. I will discover soon enough. And she went up the stairs to find her daughter in the long gallery.

Here, however, there was no sign of Miranda; only Lady Catherine, at her *petit point*, sat near the fire – just built up since the sudden inclemency in the weather – and Miss Bingley, beside her, who, Elizabeth recalled with foreboding, was due only to depart when her brother Charles and his family went to Yorkshire, on the following day. Miss Bingley, Elizabeth had often remarked to Jane, possessed all the skill of the presentiment of misfortune of a raven; and it seemed to the mistress of Pemberley, distraught as she was, that Miss Bingley gave a croak – which sounded very much like malicious laughter – at Elizabeth's entry into the room.

"Mr Darcy is at Kympton," said Lady Catherine, as her nephew's wife came up to her. "He oversees the new town; and considers the proposition of a railway station, so I believe."

"It was not so many years ago",' said Miss Bingley, "that the parson at Kympton suffered an apoplexy and was rendered quite fatuous; and his mother, as she went to assist him, tripped and fell in the kitchen and tipped a pan of scalding water all down her face and hands!"

Elizabeth did not reply to this, but she felt that Mr Darcy had made his plan to go to Kympton for a good reason.

"And there is trouble at the dairy," said Miss Bingley, who was unable to resist darting a gleeful glance at her rival of so many years past. "Miranda has gone to see it – a cow died, giving birth, and the herd stampeded in the thunderstorm!"

"Gracious!" said Elizabeth faintly, and she sat down near Lady Catherine, for want of anything else to do.

"I permitted Mr Roper to arrange the dinner, in your absence at Matlock," said Lady Catherine. "For I must inform you, dear Mrs Darcy, that we did not know when you would return, when the storm became so close overhead. Nor did I approve of the potted salmon you had decreed – it is not a fish that agrees with me at all – and I asked of Mr Roper that he countermand it, and substitute a good dish of boiled beef."

"You are of course welcome to change the receipts as well, Lady Catherine," said Elizabeth in a sharp tone, rising to her feet. "I do not believe Mr Darcy would approve, in his absence, of Mr Roper interfering with the arrangements. I am most surprised at the liberties he apparently feels free to take!"

"But, my dear Mrs Darcy," said Miss Bingley, as Elizabeth, aware all of a sudden of her wet cloak and of an immense fatigue, after the events of the day, made her way to the door of the long gallery, and to the staircase that would take her to her own bedchamber at last, "Mr Roper is heir to Pemberley, now. Lady Sophia has informed us of the necessary steps poor Mr Darcy has had to take. Surely the next in line may be permitted at least to visit the kitchens when Mr and Mrs Darcy are both away? Mr Roper has been kind enough to suggest a very fine Tokay – which I have never known you to serve at Pemberley, dear Elizabeth! Surely we can accept Mr Roper's kind offer without causing distress?"

Twenty-eight

Elizabeth's restraint and manners were much admired, at dinner, by her sister Jane, and her aunt and uncle Gardiner; for the knowledge, which every person in the room shared, but which could not be spoken of, openly, of the disinheriting of Edward, hung heavy over the table, and Lady Catherine appeared the sole diner with a hearty enjoyment of the beef. Thomas Roper, Elizabeth thought on several occasions, might receive a jab from her knife, if he continued at great length to expound on the glories of Egypt; Miss Bingley remarked in an innocent tone that the eyes of the trout handed round at table recalled to her the eyes of a dead child she had seen drowned in the pond at Barlow; and Mr Falk, remarking that he had thought little of the nuptial mass in the chapel, informed the assembly of his reply to the Archbishop of York, when that dignitary, on a visit to Pemberley, had invited him to attend evening service, that "once is orthodox, twice is puritanical".

The meal was long, Lady Catherine's method of eating the joint most repellent to Elizabeth; and the reflection that both the Gardiners and the Bingleys would be gone tomorrow filled her with a profound melancholy. Darcy would stay at Kympton as long as it pleased him. If he returned to Pemberley – as he must of course one day – it would be to find his marriage destroyed. Apart from this, all confidence in him, as steward to the land and the great house, would be much diminished in the locality – for a man who could not rear his son to accept his responsibilities must lack in the manly virtues for which Mr Darcy had so long in the county been extolled.

As for Elizabeth, she could feel no interest now in the opinions of neighbours and acquaintances. She had failed, in the nurture of her child; he was cast out from his rightful place; and, even if a part of her could accept that this was an eventuality for which they had all been prepared, she knew she never could forgive Darcy for permitting her to suffer humiliation at the hands of Miss Bingley – who beamed at the company at large, and complimented Thomas Roper on his selection of wines.

Jane, seeing the misery in Elizabeth's eyes, pressed her hand under the table, and said in a low voice that tonight, whatever might befall, they would not hear Miss de Bourgh on the pianoforte; and Elizabeth, as she gave a wan smile at this, reflected on Lady Catherine's often reiterated boast that Rosings was not in entail to a male heir – and therefore would go to her daughter Anne, when the time came. Elizabeth knew, as everyone must, in every part of the estate, that Miranda would make the perfect proprietor of Pemberley, and that this could never be. It was galling to see Miss de Bourgh – whose delicate health had not improved over all these years, remaining, like her piano playing, at a most uncertain level – as she toyed with her food, and answered her mother in a quiet voice. Why should she come into her home and estate – and Miranda not come into hers? Yet, as Elizabeth also well knew, Lady Catherine's boasts became increasingly out of touch with the reality of the situation, as Anne grew older and refused to marry. She had a reputation for turning away suitors; and now, so it was said by Mrs Hurst and her sister Miss Bingley, there was no one at all. What would befall Rosings, then?

"My dear Elizabeth," said her aunt Gardiner, as she saw the effort with which her niece kept her composure the length of the interminable repast, "let us assure you that we will care for the boy. Edward may lodge with us; now we have removed to a very quiet part of the country, he may continue his studies, or take up a profession – and we will be only too glad to give what we may, in the situation."

Elizabeth's eyes filled with tears, but these she wiped away before Miss Bingley or Lady Catherine could turn towards her. It was a blessing that the Gardiners, who did not stand on ceremony, and did not keep to the etiquette of the old school, as did the de Bourghs, and their imitators, the Bingley sisters, were able to bring out the subject uppermost in each mind, and not care for the consequences. They would speak of Edward, if they wished; he was not dead and buried yet; and the relief, to Elizabeth, almost caused her to break down completely.

"Yes, Lizzy," said Jane – remarking on the colour in her sister's cheeks, and her relief at the airing of the forbidden topic of her beloved child – "all will be well, you shall see! Edward will lodge with aunt and uncle Gardiner, in Lincoln; and you shall visit him, and his life and prospects will grow with him, into prosperity and fulfilment!"

"I trust Mr Darcy will consent to a railway track across the land at Pemberley," said Mr Roper. "I am all for progress; I intend to stand for Parliament myself, when the time comes – "

"Not as a Whig, Mr Roper, I do hope," said Lady Catherine, who now had her teeth deep in a custard.

"My dear Lady Catherine," said Mr Roper, "we must all move with the times! Reform is the order of the day! Pemberley runs to the old rhythms; it will not do at all, you know. Partly responsible, of course" – and here, the reprehensible Mr Roper cast a glance at Elizabeth, at the foot of the table, as if she were already as much a part of the past as her discarded son – "part of the trouble is the old bailiff here, Mr Gresham. He has the ideas and beliefs of a medieval tiller – he should be the first to go!"

Elizabeth caught Jane's eye, and coloured violently. The old man was loved at Pemberley – he was already considered to be on his death-bed – and Darcy, who had been so gentle and comprehending once, of the trials of humanity, as taught him by his wife and daughter, had permitted the aged estate manager to remain in his important and difficult position.

"There was a rick-burning last year at a farm not three miles from here," announced Mr Roper, though he had most definitely not been present, and Mrs Darcy could reasonably be supposed to have been in the locality. "It was quite incorrect of Mr Gresham to turn a blind eye to such monstrous insubordination!"

"I thought you proclaimed your intention of standing as a Liberal, Mr Roper," said Jane in a quiet voice.

"Indeed, indeed, Mrs Bingley. But if you were to ask me what would I do about this slavery business, if I had my way – I would be bound to reply I would do nothing at all. I would have left it all alone. It is a pack of nonsense. There always have been slaves in the most civilised countries – the Greeks, the Romans . . ."

"Very true, Mr Roper," said Lady Catherine, who now embarked on the dissecting of a jam tartlet.

"When a man is determined by his own inclination to act or not to act in a particular manner, he invariably sets about devising an argument by which he may justify himself to himself for the line he is about to pursue," said Mr Falk.

A good while later, Lady Catherine rose, and led the ladies from the dining-parlour; and Elizabeth had no choice but to follow.

Twenty-nine

There was little sleep to be had, that night, for Elizabeth; and as she lay awake, and heard the storm high above the house, and then its slow progress to the west, she pondered all the faults that had been hers, in her years as Mrs Darcy, wife of the master of Pemberley and mother of the heir. Had she truly been too indulgent with the boy? Had he, even, deserved his banishment, as Darcy believed he had? Was there something – and here Elizabeth tossed and turned, in the bed which once was wide enough for a man and wife, but now seemed too constricting for her alone – was there something left out in all this story, something she did not know?

It would not be possible, in all the years of loveless marriage that lay ahead, to believe Darcy again, when he said he told her the truth. He had concealed from her one matter so grave that he was certainly capable of holding back more. Edward had perhaps lost him a fortune – and he did not own to it. The estates in Wales were safe – but were there other debts, which threatened to ruin Pemberley, and to destroy the inheritance altogether? But Elizabeth could not think what these could be, other than the debts to tradesmen run up by all young rakes with money to throw about – and, whether she cared to accept Edward in this light, he had proved himself to outshine his peers, in folly. There was no answer to the question – it was probable that Darcy had had to reach some compromise with the father of a lad who had inveigled Edward into his disastrous gambling – but here, again, Elizabeth, with all her honesty, had to admit she could see wickedness in others, and not in her son – and that this was not the first time she had deceived herself in this way.

Morning, when it came, was dull, with rain rendering the roads all but impassable; but Elizabeth's ardent hope, that her sister would not then be able to travel back to Yorkshire, was disappointed by Charles Bingley's insistence on their return, for he had business to attend to. The Gardiners also departed, with further offers of assistance to Elizabeth, to care for Edward if the need should arise; and soon she found herself at Pemberley with only Lady Catherine and Miss de Bourgh, at their embroidery in a small sitting-room, and Mrs Reynolds to confer with on the meals which must succeed each other in this house, as in all such houses, day after day, whether there was trouble and scandal in the family or not.

Today, the task was particularly tiring, for Mrs Reynolds's covert sympathy was hard to bear; and Elizabeth soon excused herself from the kitchens, taking with her calves-foot jelly for old Mr Gresham, whom she would visit today – and deciding, in her heart, that she went for no other reason than to see the loyal bailiff and his wife. That his son might be there, she discounted entirely: there had been talk, in the servants' hall, as she went by, of Mr Gresham's departure for London; and she felt herself free, if solitary once again, as she walked through the park, basket in hand. These were her duties; she was known and loved at Pemberley for performing them with such frankness and compassion; and it did her good, walking in air that breathed of recent rain and promised more, to recall her own role here, which would go unchanged despite the misdemeanours of her son.

Hastening feet just behind her caused Elizabeth to turn her head as she approached the low gate and hedged front garden of the bailiff's house. Mr Roper, to her intense annoyance, had followed and caught up with her here – and from his excited manner, and his insistence in thrusting into her arms a large bouquet of arum lilies from her own greenhouse, she saw she would not be capable of persuading him of her need for calm and privacy, on a visit to an old man, gravely ill.

"My dear Mrs Darcy – Elizabeth – "

Elizabeth explained that she went to see Mr Gresham; she thanked Mr Roper for the flowers, but it was best that he return to the house – "for have you not the chaise ordered at four o'clock, Mr Roper? I did believe you would be going from Pemberley today."

"No, no, Elizabeth – I may address you thus, I know, in memory of your dear sister, my late spouse Mary! I hope not to go from Pemberley until my most heartfelt desires are satisfied – and it is for you alone, Elizabeth, to set me free from the torment of refusal, at so great and propitious a juncture in my life!"

Elizabeth asked him what he could possibly mean. Old Mrs Gresham now looked down from the upper window, and smiled a greeting to Mrs Darcy, who had come from the house, as she had indeed been eagerly awaited; though Elizabeth saw the old woman's smile go from her face at the sight of Mr Roper, bulging eyes and sheaf of lilies lending an air of near-insanity to an appearance already unprepossessing in the extreme.

"I come to request your approval, dearest Elizabeth, to my proposal of marriage to your daughter Miranda."

Elizabeth's first act on hearing these words was to burst out laughing; but, seeing that Mr Roper was in deadly earnest, she went pale, and took hold of the bars of the gate, to steady herself.

"What do you say, Mr Roper? It is quite out of the question, what you ask. I would appreciate your further silence on the subject, for I do not wish to hear it."

With this, Elizabeth pressed on the latch of the gate and went in; but Mr Roper, with his foot, impeded the closing of the gate behind her, and stopped her once more on the path.

"I have spoken with Miranda. She was most civil; she said I should speak to you, as her mother; and indeed the dear girl is right, for at seventeen years old she is much influenced by her mother, and rightly so."

"I see," said Elizabeth, smiling this time at the ruse

employed by her daughter. "I shall certainly answer for her, Mr Roper! The answer must be No – a hundred times No!"

Mr Roper now drew himself up to his full height. "Madam, you may regret such an attitude, one day. You will wish to be provided for at Pemberley, I have little doubt. When I am master here I wish to support the mother of my bride, in the style – "

"Please, Mr Roper," said Elizabeth, for she felt deathly cold, and a light rain had begun to fall, which brought old Mrs Gresham bustling down to open the door and usher her in. "Do not mention this subject again!"

"I fear it will be mentioned daily, until the time of the marriage," said Mr Roper, stiffly. "I regret only that you have shown your animosity to a celebration of nuptials generally considered to be a perfect solution to the problems now besetting Pemberley. Lady Catherine is all for it, as I must inform you – "

"You surprise me," said Elizabeth.

"And Mr Darcy has given his consent to the union."

"I do not believe you!" The words were out before Elizabeth could help it; the loyalty to the man she had married still lay buried in her; and the thought that she had been betrayed once again, and in a manner even more abhorrent to her than the disinheriting of Edward, was beyond her capacities for credulity.

"I beg your pardon, Mrs Darcy," said Mr Roper, bowing low as Mrs Gresham urged poor Mrs Darcy to come in out of the wet; "Mr Darcy's words to me show perfectly his understanding of my good intentions."

"*Your* good intentions?" cried Elizabeth, for the contemplation of Miranda imprisoned with this man was too vile now for her to express. "How dare you, Mr Roper?"

"Mr Darcy informed me that he liked to imagine his daughter at Pemberley, when he is gone – I fear his affections for his daughter are greater than yours, Elizabeth. He said it seemed practical to him that Miranda should be offered such an opportunity."

With these words, Mr Roper walked sharply out of the gate, which swung shut behind him. Elizabeth now followed old Mrs Gresham up to the sickbed – but, apart from the consolation of discovering that Mr Gresham's condition had been much exaggerated by Lady Sophia, there was little now on the horizon that could give claim to a desire on her own part to remain alive. Miranda marry Mr Roper! It was intolerable – yet, for all her feelings, Mrs Darcy was as kind and gentle with the old bailiff as she was expected to be; and was first to comment that the stampede of her herd last night, in the storm, must not be laid at his door – for he could scarcely have known, when still so poorly, that it would have been better to shut up the cows in the dairy than leave them out in the fields.

Thirty

Elizabeth walked back to Pemberley, when her visit was done, and refused the offer of Mrs Gresham to call her son – for he remained with them, to comfort his father – and set up a gig to convey her there.

She had too much to consider, and the need to be alone was paramount; Mr Gresham would only confuse her, at this most distressing time; and it rained not at all, though her own neglect to keep away from the trees resulted in sudden waterfalls, from leaves and branches, which ran down her neck and caused her to shiver all the more.

Now was the time she must look back on her years with Darcy, and see him for the man he really was. A monster, a tyrant – and his wealth and position had concealed the fact, very probably, just as much from her as it had from his whole court of flatterers, servitors and those who worked the estate. He was a petty king, no more; and just what her mother, Mrs Bennet, had liked in him – that he would give her horses and carriages and jewels – must be the reason for her marrying him.

She was the hypocrite, not her mother. Had she not known in her heart that Darcy was her foe, not her friend; for what friend would take a child, so loved, and throw him into the darkness of disinheritance? And was not Charles Bingley, who confided his every thought and action to her sister Jane, the husband she would have preferred – to a man so secretive, so prone to violent rage occasioned even by an evening of boredom – that she had as much as she could do, to win him back to good humour again? The answer must be that Jane had all the good fortune she merited, and Elizabeth received her just deserts; and as she walked on, allowing the dripping trees to add their water to the tears on her cheeks, she recalled her father's words to her, on the occasion of Mr Darcy's asking her hand in marriage, in an age that seemed so far removed to her now, at Longbourn. "Lizzy" – and here Mr Bennet's exact timbre of voice came back so clearly to her, she had to stop under an oak, in sight now of the windows of Pemberley, but alone in the great expanse of the park – "let me advise you to think better of it." And Elizabeth saw him in the library at Longbourn, gazing at her with a concern which could not be concealed by his habitual levity. "I know your disposition, Lizzy. I know that you could be neither happy nor respectable, unless you truly esteemed your husband; unless you looked up to him as a superior. Your lively talents would place you in the greatest danger in an unequal marriage. You could scarcely escape discredit and misery . . ."

Here was discredit and misery indeed, thought Elizabeth with a heavy heart. Hers was indeed an unequal marriage. How could she esteem her husband now – when he had banished her son, and would marry her daughter to Thomas Roper? As she wept and walked on, Elizabeth thought of all the talk of the new age that was on them – of reform and progress and the boasts of men – and she could conclude only that there was no reform for *her* – no reform or progress for Miranda, either – and in her heart she hardened against Darcy, and resolved to withdraw every last inch of affection or loyalty to him. He had betrayed her; and now she had recourse to think again of Mr Bennet – laughing at the very idea of her accepting Mr Collins, when he had come on an identical mission, as heir to Longbourn. "My father did not need such words as progress or reform; he did not approve of my marrying anyone I did not wish to marry." Elizabeth's thoughts continued. "Even if it were Mr Darcy, with ten thousand a year." That she now regretted her decision was too pathetic to confess – and she increased her speed, as rain began to fall again, and the dismal aspect of the park became oppressive. She had her life to live out here – but she must find Miranda, and save her from the ruin of *hers*, without further delay.

Mr Gresham made his appearance just as a fine mist settled over the trees – and, as both he and Elizabeth were now coming towards each other in an open and deserted part of the grounds, there was little they could do to get out of each other's way. Elizabeth smiled, and went even faster; Mr Gresham was, as she could see, downcast, and wore an air of embarrassment; but good manners dictated they stop and exchange sentiments on the subject of the health of Mr Gresham's father, and the certainty of his full recovery within a matter of days.

"Thank you for taking your gifts to my mother and father," said Gresham, in a low voice. "And I do beg you, if you need assistance, in any matter concerning your son and his misfortunes – you have only to inform me."

Elizabeth felt a lifting of the spirits so great, at the subject coming out in the open, and at Mr Gresham's offer to do all he could for the boy, that half her fears seemed to dispel. For Gresham she could trust – he was not against all the dearest wishes of her heart, like her husband – and she would very much like him to come to the assistance of Edward, as she told him, in a voice that wavered but was filled with joy.

It was the first time for so long that she had felt at peace with herself, as she went with Gresham along the last stretch of the garden to the south door of Pemberley, Elizabeth reflected as she went inside and climbed the stairs to the long gallery, that she could forgive and forget the past, their ill-fated meeting in the woods, and his transparent gaze, at the marriage of Colonel Fitzwilliam. She had a friend; and she could one day love him, so she could hope – if he permitted Edward a right to life still, as he did.

Part Four

Thirty-one

The next days at Pemberley passed without storms or disasters, as might be hoped for, now Miss Bingley had departed; and before long Lady Catherine and her daughter made their farewells, accompanied by Mr Roper. Miranda had been at Barlow since the day of Elizabeth's visit to old Mr Gresham – there was an outbreak of sickness there, among the cattle, and her uncle, Charles Bingley, had come to depend on the girl's forthright good sense and dedication to the veterinary skills in which she had been trained, on the farms at Pemberley.

The house was empty and still; and gradually, as Elizabeth made her way from morning conference with Mrs Reynolds to the old schoolroom where Mr Falk was happy to regale her with tales of Edward – for he loved the boy, there was little doubt of it – she began to feel her future unfurl before her, and the past unravel also, making altogether a new picture of her life.

There had been faults in the marriage; it could not be denied; and there were grave faults in Darcy, still, for he was more often proud than humble, and he saw those lower than he as another species entirely from the heirs to Pemberley. But, most of all, Elizabeth saw her own need to grow – away from the impulsive, strong-willed young woman who had taken these qualities to her marriage and had thought them expressions of maturity and independence – towards a state where she could find herself sufficient to herself, in a world where Darcy ruled as far as the horizon and beyond.

He would have the upper hand, for as long as they were wed.

And wed they must remain, whether she liked it or not: he would dictate the terms, and she must in all passivity watch her daughter, as strong-willed and spirited as she, subjugate her life to Mr Roper; for Darcy would ensure the alternatives were too dismal, even for a girl such as Miranda, to decide to lose Pemberley. Edward would count for nothing – and Elizabeth would be permitted to see him from time to time. There would be grandchildren – but here Elizabeth shrugged her shoulders and went over to the mirror, in her room with long windows that looked out over the perfection of the park and grounds. She would be consoled by this, she knew; but she was aware too that she had youth in her yet, and vigour, and a hope that had been cruelly crushed. Her new lesson, of detachment and indifference, of kindness to all those who needed her, but of a life without sensuality, without pleasure – and her very vigour gave her the love of pleasant things, of joy and activity, that her husband had always loved in her – was for now too hard to bear. She saw herself walled up at Pemberley, as faithless wives or abandoned, forgotten daughters had been in days gone past – and, in the unending cycle of days and seasons and family members and visitors fed and heard, she saw her own death stark and clear. She *did* need to change – but her life would never change, so how could *she*? Round and round went these thoughts – and the slow return of the glorious seasonal weather, the bright beds of lavender and sweet-scented blooms visible from her window, came more as a taunt to her powerlessness and her imprisoned state than as a symbol of the happy years she had known, while bringing up her young family and making her garden bloom.

A letter came, from Jane at Barlow. Her family thanked their aunt Lizzy for their happy stay at Pemberley. They had all their old corners and hiding-places there; little Joshua had been quite astonished at the Jersey herd, and Emily had sworn to practise at the piano more, after the evening with Miss de Bourgh. Elizabeth smiled, at the kind thought that lay behind the letter – but it wounded her, too, that her sister lived still in the world of family happiness, while she was cast out, with Edward, and would never accord such importance to the daily things of life as dear Jane did, with her talk of the dog upsetting the music stand and all the pages flying about, and their son home soon on leave – and what would they give him to eat?

Miranda was in high spirits – so Jane went on to say – and she and Charles had never known her happier. As if charmed by her cure, the cattle in the park at Barlow recovered; the weather was so fine again, she began to think of water and envy her sister the trip to Venice. "Think of it, Lizzy, and you deserve it – after the wedding and all the to-ing and fro-ing you have had to do! Darcy, who holds you more dear than his own life, will take you out to the sea, from the Grand Canal – Oh, I wish I could persuade Charles to take me too, but he has much to oversee on the farm this year . . .", and so on.

Elizabeth sighed and put away the letter. She was doubly pierced now; for to hear that Miranda was well and contented with her choice – and this must surely mean no less – was to wonder at the stranger she had nursed all these years. The girl was her father's daughter – but she had been the image of Elizabeth when she was small – and the mother's heart ached for her, that she put land and wealth and position above true happiness. Miranda had chosen Pemberley; but then, as it grieved Elizabeth even further to confess, her own choice of husband, which had come from love and not – as she had laughingly said to Jane, at the time – from her first sight of the park at Pemberley, had combined all the grandeur of estate and name, with a real passion; and it was now in ashes.

It was very likely better, Elizabeth concluded, as she walked on the lawn and looked out on the lake, like polished steel under a cloudless blue sky, to marry for convenience, after all. And Miranda had come from Pemberley; she loved the place more, perhaps, than she could love any man. She had chosen rightly; and she was happy. But it was hard for Elizabeth, when she looked back on her own past, as Mr Bennet's daughter at Longbourn, and Mr Collins's proposal of marriage, to forget her own scorn and indignation, and Mr Bennet's reassurance that she need pay no attention to her suitor, even if an entail meant he would one day inherit Longbourn. But then Elizabeth had not loved Longbourn as her daughter loved Pemberley. There was no comparison between the romance and splendour of the one, and the constrictions of the other – and, besides, Mrs Bennet's nerves had had so debilitating an effect, on her two eldest daughters at least, that fond memories of childhood were not so plentiful for Elizabeth as they now proved to be for her daughter. Miranda had run free, here. As wife of Mr Roper, she would have the place as much to herself as before.

Thoughts of her own life as a girl were interrupted by the arrival of an express – it was from Elizabeth's sister, Lydia – and she wondered at the difference, not for the first time, between Jane, who personified all that was calm, accepting and radiant, and Lydia, who had never once, in all Elizabeth's years at Pemberley, written without the stating of an urgent request. With foreboding, Elizabeth took the letter up. The address was Meryton Lodge; and she frowned.

Dear Lizzy,

I do trust your glorious celebrations for the marriage of Colonel Fitzwilliam went off very well. I am at Mama's house, as you can see – and I write because Mama was most distressed to receive your letter, enquiring after her acquaintanceship with Lady Harcourt. Indeed, poor Mama has a migraine now; and Mrs Long has a new medicament for it, but the doctor informs us it is no more than an old wives' remedy and may make her headache worse.

She wishes to assure you – as do I, dear Lizzy – that neither of us has any intention of seeing Lady Harcourt again.

You may have heard that Mama was invited to a wedding, of a relation of Lady Harcourt – and as I am so very poor, Lizzy, and stuck down in Pymore with such a brood, and Wickham, who was dispossessed of the stipend promised him by old Mr Darcy, all those years ago, can scarcely make ends meet – in short, Mama had the idea that I should attend the wedding with her. I do not care for London, as you may know – it is intensely fatiguing, and Wickham and I have so large an acquaintance there, that it would be foolhardy in the extreme to give out that one intended to go – so I went incognito, you might say – and if it had not been for my own presence of mind, I dare say Mama and I might never have got home at all!

The carriage in which we had been brought to London was taken away from the main thoroughfare and down into the mean streets of Soho. The coachman, and a footman who was no such thing – grabbed poor Mama and myself – and you know I hurt my arm when the children fell from the swing in the orchard, it needs a doctor, or I may well lose it altogether, Lizzy, but I cannot find the money for one – and hustled us into a low building where it was very dark, and Mama nearly fainted from the candle smoke.

You know, Lizzy, how often I wish we were more welcome under your roof at Pemberley! Wickham is prepared to forget the grievous harm done him by your husband, now they are brothers-in-law! – but it is so many years since we were with you there, and had the pleasure of seeing your children, that I would have been hard put to swear the young man standing a few feet from us *was* your son, Edward –

"Edward," said Elizabeth aloud.

He is not very much taller than when we last saw him, as a child – so at first I could not be certain, Lizzy. He – Edward – stood at a makeshift altar – there were so many candles there, the smoke all but blinded us – and by his side was a young woman. Lady Harcourt came up to us and showed us the young woman, who had a painted face, and said this was her relation, and the marriage to which she had invited Mama and myself was about to take place, but a little different, doubtless, from what we had expected when we came to town!

165

"Edward at a marriage – at his own – " thought Elizabeth, not believing yet, and afraid to re-read the letter so soon.

Mama was overcome – Lady Harcourt said she wished Mama to witness the marriage of her grandson. After the ceremony, they would go to Scotland, so she said, and there they would be wed in the eyes of the law. She tried to pull us forward, but at that moment Mama fainted, and it was all I could do, with the assistance of a most unappealing man, who claimed to be an usher, to transport her the length of the room.

Elizabeth, who had been standing at the window to read Lydia's letter, now went to sit abruptly in her chair, by the desk where each day she filled out her agenda, for Mrs Reynolds, to ensure the smooth organisation of life in a great house such as Pemberley. She felt herself in the smoky room; she suffered for Edward, and then abominated his foolishness; she wondered, in her agony, where he was now. Finally, as steps came up the stairs, and the visit of Mrs Reynolds was imminent, she laid her head down on the surface of the desk, and wept.

"I took poor Mama out into the street," Lydia's letter continued, when Elizabeth raised her head again and held the letter close to her:

I took Mama, so she might recover, to Mr Darcy's house in Holland Park – here we rested, before returning to Hertfordshire once more.

How many times I have said I wished to see the interior of your fine house in Holland Park since it has been refashioned, Lizzy! It is magnificent indeed! But I do not believe you comprehend the increase in value of the snuff-boxes and cameos which you have on display there! They are not well shown – and besides, I know several gentlemen who are connoisseurs, who would give a fine price for them. I have them here, Lizzy – by your leave – and I will inform you of the outcome of my approaches.

Please do not fret, therefore – I am quite well, though

the summer is oppressive at Meryton. Mama's migraine as a constant topic of conversation will very likely drive me back to Dorset sooner than I intended!

Yours loving sister,
Lydia

Thirty-two

Elizabeth rose from her desk; and, despite Mrs Reynolds's surprise – which she could not conceal, for all her years as housekeeper – made a brief announcement that there would be no conference today, on the subject of provisions and repasts to be planned for the coming week; and went at speed down the stairs and out of the house.

It was a bright day, but with more of a touch of gold in the air than midsummer; and Elizabeth found herself, before she could look either side of her, at the park gates, which led to the road to Threlwell, the nearest town and two or three miles distant from the main entrance to the gate.

For the first time since she had come here as the wife of Fitzwilliam Darcy, she did not look back at the house, before leaving the gates and entering a road overhung by ancient beeches. She did not wish to turn – to turn once would prove fatal, to her need to find her own thoughts, and compose herself for the future. She did not stop to catch a last glimpse of the noble façade, stern grey stone with porticoes and pediments that gave such grace and symmetry to the whole, that to live there was to breathe the spirit of harmony; she would not be deceived again by the balance and sheer sense of the place, set in a hollow where a stream gave endless murmuring relief from onerous thoughts, and wooded hills protected house and outbuildings from storm and wind.

For now she knew this was not the home of justice and careful consideration. Here were prejudice and loathing; love had no place here: order and obedience were king, and the greed that keeps men holding, come what may, to land and money. She would not believe again that pleasant rooms, and polite talk, and pictures and glades and fine grounds were the measure of a fair society. They were the very opposite, she now understood; truth could be found only with the poor and disinherited, who must speak out, to gain their own voice, or lie still another century, to be trampled on by their masters. Pemberley was an emblem of all that was false, and untrue – and she would not look, as she left the gates, through the hedges of copper beech, their old leaves still dying from last winter, that made up the polite boundary to Mr Darcy's home. If she came again to this house, where she had thought herself so happy, it would be in another spirit, and with quite other demands to those that had been spoken in the past. But she did not think she would come – and she did not think she would be heard, if she were to speak. Those who enjoyed the favours of Pemberley learned to be silent, early; or were born to an acquiescence to the old order of things. Even Miranda did not question the accession, here – for there was a royal feel to the whole place – and Elizabeth hated it all the more for that, as she walked at a brisk rate along the road to town.

That there was much reason to feel shame, she well knew. Mrs Bennet – her own mother – had brought the Darcy family to ruin, doubtless as Lady Catherine had prophesied she would, one day. She had attended the wedding of her grandson! She had been duped; and now she appeared a scoundrel, an associate of a woman with a reputation for acts bordering on the criminal. She had been an idiot – and Darcy could be said to be correct, from the very first, that there was insanity in Mrs Bennet's family, as well as a distinct lack of the results of upbringing expected from a gentleman's daughter. Darcy had been informed, Elizabeth supposed, of the attendance of his mother-in-law at this shameful occasion. He had warned their son that he must quit the company of Lady Harcourt and her associates, on pain of permanent exile from his birthright, should he be discovered with them again. And Edward had disobeyed – flagrantly – he had gone straight back there; and, fool that he was, he had married some bawd put up to act as bait for a blackmailer, as emblem of perpetual embarrassment and dishonour to the family.

Elizabeth reflected, as she went, that in past days she would have suffered more, at the exposure of her mother's ridiculous credulity – and also of Lydia's disingenuousness and stupidity. She would have been contrite – as she had been at the time of her first acquaintance with Darcy, on learning his role as saviour to Lydia, in the ill-considered elopement with Captain Wickham; and she would have known herself at fault, that she had judged Mr Darcy without knowing the facts of his generous interference – or of Wickham's true nature, as revealed to both Darcy and his cousin Colonel Fitzwilliam. Mrs Bennet was an easy conduit for shame – Elizabeth was aware of that. There had been the matter of Colonel Kitchiner, which had proved distasteful in the extreme, and had polluted the shades of Pemberley, as Lady Catherine had predicted. This time, however, her mother had surpassed herself – for what was an unsuitable admirer, whom Mrs Bennet had admittedly encouraged soon after finding herself a widow, when compared with the eager striking up of an acquaintance such as Lady Harcourt? How could anyone, other than her mother, with her nerves, and her recent espousal of the migraine, be so blind as to be deceived by a woman of ill repute?

Yet, Elizabeth reflected, her mother had known a hard life – far harder than Mr Darcy's, certainly – and had suffered the impatience of her husband and the lack of sympathy of her daughters for close on a quarter of a century. When a guest at Pemberley – and inevitably at a seasonal occasion which also saw Lady Catherine de Bourgh under the roof – Mrs Bennet had been slighted so frequently, and with such care and nicety, that only Elizabeth had felt her cheeks burn, in mortification. To see her mother unaware of the insults she received at the hands of Mrs Hurst, and other ladies of the county, doubtless encouraged in teasing Mrs Darcy's mother, as a way of passing an agreeable evening at Pemberley, had sometimes been too much to tolerate – but Darcy, in the way of men, had noticed nothing, and, after trying a few times to explain the wiles and games of his guests' pursuit of their prey, she had let go of the subject, and suffered in silence, or, if she was present, with Jane.

Now Darcy blamed her mother on two counts, it seemed! Her family was mad, for one; and, for the other, she had approved the wedding of Edward. Elizabeth felt only indignation at this assumption of the reasoning of her mother – for surely she could not have known where she went, in London, or even why, overcome as she had been by the supposed grandeur of Lady Harcourt.

Elizabeth was aware she banished all thought of the future of her son from her mind, as she walked to Threlwell, on the lane they had walked so often together, when he was a boy and in need of amusement, or a visit to the weekly fair. Her mind dwelt only on Darcy's humiliating assumption of her mother's liability in this sorry business. Edward's most recent behaviour, as so many times before, was impossible for her to contemplate. She did not see what could become of him, now that he had acted with such rashness and impetuosity, but she did not believe the lad could be lawfully wed – not at his age and in such circumstances – and she found most riling of all the knowledge that Darcy must have opinions, as well as intelligence, on this, and would not share them with her. That his son had disobeyed him, and had fallen into the clutches of this unsavoury woman, was reprehensible – that she could see. But she suspected, at heart, that Darcy found simply another reason to disinherit his son; he had wanted to since the boy was seven years old; and along the way there were grounds for despising the silliness and vulgarity of Mrs Bennet, for good measure. His power over his wife increased, with every fault or folly committed by her son, or by her mother; Elizabeth knew this now, and she had not known it so clearly before. She would find a way to a new life; even if it meant estrangement from Darcy, she could find a way to esteem herself, if she could not esteem *him*.

Thirty-three

The outskirts of Threlwell showed more animation than was usual, and a vastly increased number of people in the crowd for market day, even in the height of summer; and Elizabeth found herself swept along the narrow, cobbled streets into the square. There was something about to happen: she felt the excitement, but did not feel apprehensive, though she received many curious glances as she went. There was a horse fair, perhaps – or a travelling circus of clowns and acrobats, such as Edward had loved as a child. But the air of dedication and anticipation was greater than that; and if, for one moment, she had a sickening sense of a mob going in search of the punishment of a felon, she knew just as rapidly that this, also, was not the mood of the crowd. Justice was indeed sought after – but by a new and different means.

The centre of the square was draped in flags and banners; and here, on a high wooden platform, stood three figures, each waiting for the mass of people to find a place in the wide square. Here livestock and booths for cotton and household goods could normally be found, on a Saturday; but that trading was not on the minds of the people of Threlwell today was evident by the pushing into corners of the usual places of commerce, and the concentration on the tall personage who came forward on the podium. That this, as became clear to Elizabeth as she was propelled forward by the throng, was Mr Gresham was acknowledged by the shouting of his name and the excited round of applause which greeted his appearance. He began to speak: an eager, determined silence followed his words; and only the cry of a child, or the scuffling of dogs by the Corn Exchange at the far side of the square, interrupted his raptly attended peroration.

Elizabeth listened, too, with a wish to understand, to encourage and assist all the aims that the son of the agent at Pemberley now proclaimed. She knew she witnessed a new moment; a moment in history that would pass by the great estate where she was chatelaine – and, if it did, it might well be the worse, for all incumbents there. The people – and she recognised the faces of tenant farmers, and of estate workers at Pemberley, counting that there were more of these in search of a new standing in life than there were small tradesmen, or shopkeepers – would have change, and they would not wait longer for it. There was a great need for equality, for independence – and there was exhilaration at the breaking free of the system of pocket boroughs, which, as Elizabeth was well aware, were tacitly condoned by Mr Darcy and his peers. There was the urgent necessity for continuing reform.

Elizabeth believed in the rightness of the cause; and she thought of her poor son, who must be chastised by exile from land to which the people here had more rightful claim than he – for did they not work it, night and day, week in, week out, while a young scamp had the power to dice away their livelihoods, miles to the south, in London? Should there not be a system which removed the rights of inheritance altogether? – but here, Elizabeth understood, she surpassed even Mr Gresham in her radical thoughts and new opinions. For the present, Gresham was a realist, and a careful politician; he campaigned for reform – and the people, in a swell of cheers and approval, came behind him, every one of them.

Mr Gresham saw Elizabeth in the crowd – and for a minute he paused, unable to keep his eyes from her – and others now noticed the mistress of Pemberley, and stood back a little, so she had an uncomfortable sense of isolation. This she had for many years tried to overcome, at parties and celebrations for those who worked on the estate and their wives and children, but there was no denying her apartness, from those very people she wished most to help: they appreciated her thoughtfulness and her bounty, she knew – but the gulf between them would never narrow while she was married to Mr Darcy, of Pemberley.

Now a murmur went up – and even Mr Gresham's words were drowned out by it. Two estate workers in the crowd – whose living conditions in a rural hamlet that was little better than the quarters of the animals they tended – set up a riotous mood, waved wooden posts, used for fencing the Pemberley estate; and her name went round. Darcy – it was hers, whether she would disown it or not. The fact of Elizabeth's attempts to persuade her husband that those cottages, where the men lived in squalor with a great brood of children, should be demolished and rebuilt, had gone unheard – but how should they know *that*? – or that she had cared, and had gone to old Mr Gresham to put her case, again without success. She could feel the antipathy of Threlwell as it centred on the lady of the great house – and she saw the concern, and the devotion in Mr Gresham's eyes, as he understood her agreement with his principles, and saw her desire to assist him in his crusade – while finding herself ineluctably on the other side.

Mr Gresham stepped down from the platform, and came towards the troublemakers. They respected him; and they saw the anger in his eyes, and fell quiet. Then a voice cried out – a voice about sixteen years old, Elizabeth imagined, and recognisable as the voice of a child of a labourer, Jack Martin, once one of Edward's playmates from the village at Pemberley. The voice demanded to know the whereabouts of young Master Darcy, and to be told if what was said was true – that he whored and gambled in London, while a bad year, with falling prices for livestock, could take a man to his grave, here in Threlwell. Did he prosper, then, the heir to Mr Darcy, or was he as poxy as the rest of them?

Elizabeth became paler, as laughter in the crowd rang out, and heads turned towards her. Mr Gresham she could not see – he was lost in the throng, his power and visibility for the moment gone – and she had scarcely the time to blame herself once more, for taking the young architect's moment of triumph from him, on this most momentous of days, when a taller figure approached her, from a side street behind the Exchange, and, as if in some tacit consent born of many centuries of deference, the crowd fell back to let him through.

Charles Bingley reached Elizabeth, and inclined his head – without his usual, genial manner.

"Mrs Darcy – Elizabeth?"

The silence that fell over the market square at Threlwell that day was remarkable even to the children who whined and played at the feet of their elders. For Mrs Darcy must go with her brother-in-law; she had no place here, and should not be walking about alone in this way; Mrs Darcy of Pemberley must go in a carriage, and here was such a one, as if by an act of Providence, come to carry her back to the state and pomp where, in their minds at the very least, she belonged.

Elizabeth went with Charles Bingley: she knew it would be impossible for a woman of her position to refuse to do so, publicly; and to draw attention to herself would endanger the prospects of Mr Gresham even further.

The carriage rolled back to Pemberley; and Elizabeth sat, her eyes turned to the window, to prevent her tears becoming the property of Charles Bingley.

"My dear sister," said he – and he was a good man, and concerned, she could understand. "We called at Pemberley, hoping to see you – for Jane says you are quite alone here, and it must be very dull – "

"Jane is come with you?" said Elizabeth, brightening, as they reached the gates and descended into the park, and the house, golden by now in the rays of the late sun, stood as if painted in its ornamental garden and grounds.

"I do not believe you should go as far as Threlwell without an escort," said Charles Bingley, frowning – but, before his words were out of his mouth, Elizabeth had leapt from the

176

coach and run to her sister, who stood on the steps by the west door to Pemberley.

Thirty-four

More than once, as Elizabeth sat with Jane in her boudoir, did she feel a renewed sense of the unfairness of her position; but Jane, whom she loved so well, and who was so fair and considerate in her judgements, brought her always back into silence; and even in the matter of Lydia's letter, and its unwelcome contents, the estimable Mrs Bingley had words of caution and explanation.

"Dear Lizzy – it has been hard for Darcy, too – for the letter he received, from Mr Collins . . ."

"Mr Collins?" said Elizabeth, frowning in distaste at the mention of the man who had inherited Longbourn – and had married her old friend Charlotte, the marriage finally rendering the young Miss Lucas in her invisible, the long-suffering wife of Mr Collins being all that remained of her.

"Yes – Mr Collins wrote to Mr Darcy that Mama approved this . . . this marriage of Edward and some woman cried up as Lady Harcourt's niece! That she knew well before the event that it was to take place – and she showed her invitation freely, to prove it."

"That cannot be," said Elizabeth, who saw that her sister and Mr Bingley had had confidences from Darcy which she had not; and she suffered a pang, despite advice to herself to refrain from doing so. "Do you imagine Mama can have thought she was asked to Edward's marriage, Jane? It is quite ridiculous to think so."

"Darcy believed only what he was told by Charlotte's husband," said Jane calmly. "Mr Collins's communication was a result of a confidence from Sir William Lucas, that he had come upon Edward – or he imagined it was he – in London, in the company of a young woman. This, combined with natural apprehensions after Mama's disclosure that she sent money to Lady Harcourt, caused Mr Collins to write as he did."

That is all very well, thought Elizabeth, but Darcy still does not take the trouble to think of the real nature of our mother, and the improbability of her setting off for London to see her young grandson wed, when he is not even of an age to marry!

"Mama was piqued that she was not to come to Pemberley for the marriage of Colonel Fitzwilliam," said Jane.

Yes; this time Elizabeth had grudgingly to admit she saw it all too clearly: Mrs Bennet boasted of her grand connections in London, and of an invitation to a marriage which would outdo the marriage at Pemberley, in its supposed importance.

"But Mr Collins misunderstood Mama," said Elizabeth, "I am certain of it. And Darcy did not care to discover further the truth of her meddling or otherwise – before accusing her, and cutting out Edward from his life. He believed Mr Collins! He is prejudiced, Jane, I am sorry to say it."

"And you are proud, Lizzy," said Jane in a quiet voice. "For you did not give Darcy the opportunity to inform you of a further communication – a most unpleasant one, I must say – from Lady Harcourt herself, in which she attempted to extort money from him, in return for her silence on the subject of Edward's soi-disant marriage."

Elizabeth was silent at this, but her sister observed that she bit her lip and gazed at anyone rather than her.

"Darcy refused absolutely, as you might expect. But reports of Mrs Bennet's approval did not assist matters. I see you wonder why Darcy does not come to you," Jane continued, "and ask your opinion on these contingencies, as they arise – but he must forgive you, for the wounding words you spoke to him, on his upbringing of the boy – as you must forgive him for his, on the subject of Mama."

"So he has told you of our exchange, when I returned from Matlock," said Elizabeth with some bitterness.

"He spoke with Charles. Darcy loves you, Elizabeth! He wants only to restore harmony in the family – "

"How is that possible?" cried Elizabeth, her eyes burning very brightly, as Jane recalled from times when, as sisters, they had fallen out and hurt each other with their recriminations. "He is a monster, Jane – you cannot condone his attitude to Miranda – "

"To Miranda?" said Jane, with a look of real surprise. "She is happy as the day is long, Lizzy – and I only pray you will forgive us for keeping her so long at Barlow, where she brings relief to our sick animals and joy wherever she goes!"

"Darcy has approved her marriage to Thomas Roper, Jane – has she not informed you of it? And", Elizabeth went on as Jane looked at her in astonishment, "she does not refuse the offer, not at all! It is unspeakable!" And here, as if the time that had passed without the surrender of her deepest emotions must now be compensated for, Elizabeth burst out sobbing, and could not calm until her sister's arms were around her.

"Lizzy – I would laugh if you did not cry so terribly," said Jane, when she could speak, "for Miranda would not consider marrying Mr Roper for anything in the world! Where did you get the idea, my poor Eliza?"

The reply came, in muffled tones, that Mr Roper had followed Elizabeth across the park, had told her of Darcy's approval – that he had said, in so many words, that Miranda should take the opportunity to stay all her life at Pemberley.

"My poor sister," said Jane smiling, as Elizabeth, seeing the misapprehension, if such there was, looked anxiously at her. "Mr Darcy appoints Miranda as agent at Pemberley. Old Mr Gresham is fortunately recovered from his illness – but he is weak, he cannot undertake the management of so large an estate again – "

"Agent at Pemberley?" repeated Elizabeth, whose turn it now was to be astonished.

"And, if you would permit him, he would tell you this himself," said Jane, "but he has been with us a short while, on his way to London – "

"He is in London," said Elizabeth in a dull voice.

"He may be returned to Kympton by now, Lizzy – I am sorry I should be so much more aware of the movements of Mr Darcy than yourself! But it is clear to him that Pemberley is in urgent need of new management. There is a new feeling abroad – "

"Indeed there is," said Elizabeth; and she told Jane of the meeting at Threlwell, and of Mr Gresham's success as campaigner for the new, progressive cause.

"Mr Darcy is one who can put the new agricultural methods into practice," said Jane, "for words are very fine; but the owner of land has the power to show the results of a new approach. Miranda has convinced him – "

"And what of the need for a different and improved way of life for the tenants?" said Elizabeth.

Here came a light knock at the door, and Charles Bingley stood there, smiling by way of apology for breaking into the sisters' conference.

"I am sent to enquire . . ." he began.

"What can it be?" asked Elizabeth, rising nervously. "I am needed – is someone ill?"

"Only as ill as a man with a broken heart can be expected to be," said Mr Darcy, stepping into the room – and looking remarkably fit and handsome, as Elizabeth was sorry to note.

"If I may, I will reply to your query, my loveliest Elizabeth, on the subject of the tenants and cottagers at Pemberley. It was you – and not Miranda alone – who persuaded me that we must move with the times – "

"And show kindness and respect for human equality," said Elizabeth in a firm tone, which went, however, unheard by Mr Darcy.

"Miranda will make an excellent manager here, and there will be no cause for complaint, from anyone on the estate or in any capacity at all," said Darcy with an air of finality. "But, dearest Elizabeth, I come to ask you to forgive me . . ."

Jane Bingley signalled to her husband, and the couple left the room, Jane smiling and pointing her eyes heavenward in a demand for understanding on the part of her sister, before leaving the room and running with a light tread down the stairs.

"I come from London, dearest Elizabeth, and I come at speed, for I could not live another day or night without setting eyes on you!"

"Indeed," said Elizabeth.

"Our house lacks a number of snuff-boxes and bibelots," said Darcy with a smile, "but on this occasion it contained also the traces of a visitor – a Mrs Wickham, if you care to know."

"Lydia?" exclaimed Elizabeth.

"I did not ask the servants too many questions of her provenance," said Mr Darcy, "any more than I did of the *objets de vertu* with which she appeared to have filled her bag. But I did ascertain from Mrs Blandford, who is, as you know, as respectable a housekeeper as her sister, Mrs Reynolds, at Pemberley, that Mrs Bennet had no inkling of the true nature of the marriage she was to witness at Lady Harcourt's. She was, in fact, deeply shocked, and made ill by the occasion. I beg your forgiveness, Elizabeth, for the cruel words I spoke about your mother; and pray you will grant me relief from the pain I have suffered at being apart from you!"

There was a good deal to be said, now; and Elizabeth's resolve, weaker though it might be by the minute, was still strong enough to insist on information on the future of their son, however contentious a subject, alas, this inevitably turned out to be. This time, however, there was a new understanding in the reply Darcy gave her; and, as this was accompanied by a solemn oath to share with her all the decisions on future actions taken on the part of their children, Elizabeth decided to hear him with a measure of impartiality.

"We both know, my Eliza, that Edward is not fit, at present, to sustain the load of responsibilities inherent in the position of heir to Pemberley. From Kympton I travelled to London, where I consulted my lawyers — it will be a lengthy process — but I shall find a way to end the entail here, which is the real culprit in all this, my dearest."

"End the entail?" said Elizabeth, as if she could not believe her ears — and, Jane and Charles re-entering the room at this moment, she turned to them and said the words once again.

"I must be reprehended", said Darcy gravely, "for my inability to resist informing Colonel Fitzwilliam of my intentions. I should have known that he would give the gist of my words to Lady Sophia — and that she would distort the meaning. Edward is not disinherited, as such — "

"He is not?" cried Elizabeth.

"Pemberley will be in the names of both Edward and Miranda," said Darcy — as Charles Bingley nodded approval, and Elizabeth ran to clasp Jane's hand. "Miranda will make an excellent manager, as we know — and Edward, when he is arrived at maturity, will increase his responsibility according to his success as landowner, and overseer of our estates. At present he is in the charge of the manager of the estates in Wales — and, I hope, learning that forestry is more engaging as an occupation than losing a great acreage of trees in the bottom of a dicing-cup."

Elizabeth went at last to the side of her husband — but she was now held at arm's length by him, with a laugh. "There is indeed one decision, Elizabeth, which I have had the audacity to arrive at, without you. I trust you can forgive me for it."

Elizabeth demanded what this decision could be — but she saw her sister's eyes sparkle, and turn to the picture visible through the door to her bedchamber, and at which she had gazed with such anticipation from her fourposter bed.

"We shall depart for Venice in the morning," said Mr Darcy. "But only if you permit it, Elizabeth!"

Elizabeth and Darcy were not seen at Pemberley for some weeks after this – it was not given out that they had gone away and would not return in time for the visit to Yorkshire, where the shooting season was shortly due to begin. Mr and Mrs Gardiner, who stayed there in the Darcys' absence, for Mr Gardiner to enjoy the moors and the fishing, received a letter from Elizabeth in Italy. They reported to no one other than Jane Bingley that their niece was very happy in Venice, but was looking forward to her return to Pemberley – for there was much to do, in the making of a new Italian garden, a project on which she and Mr Darcy had decided. Mr Gresham would do the design; and Mr Darcy had been required to spend some time persuading his wife of the desirability of it.

Mr Falk, who had been informed that he might stay on at Pemberley for as long as he pleased, had many anecdotes of Venetian Popes and painters to tell the happy couple, on the day they came home.

The sighting of a young man, and a woman with a child in her arms, walking up the drive at Pemberley, was kept from Mr and Mrs Darcy by the old tutor, whose sole comment, on the subject of all present and future incumbents of Pemberley, was that "neither man nor woman can be worth anything until they have discovered they are fools. This is the first step to becoming either estimable or agreeable; and, until it is taken, there is no hope. The sooner the discovery is made the better, as there is more time and power for taking advantage of it."

That Elizabeth did not look up to Mr Darcy as a superior, as Mr Bennet had decreed, was soon evident in the new management of the estate, for the increased prosperity of the tenants was entirely due to her; and that she now saw him as an equal was shown in the manner in which Darcy was encouraged to spend time alone in Wales with Edward, without his wife deciding on all the boy's occupations herself.

The wife of Colonel Fitzwilliam did not come to Pemberley, except at Christmas and other solemn occasions – for, as Mr

Darcy said, laughing, to Elizabeth one day, as they walked in the garden, "There are no half measures for Lady Sophia, I fear – it is all or nothing with her!"

The End